WONDERLAND

KIMBERLY WHEELOCK

To the eleven-year-old girl who made it her
dream to become an author:

we did it.

Wilderness camping permits, climbing permits, and park information are available at the Carbon River Ranger Station. Carbon River Road may be closed due to flooding. Call the park for current conditions.

Mount Rainier National Park
Geographic Information System
REVISED 2/06

LEGEND

- ▲ WILDERNESS TRAILSIDE CAMP
- ▲ FRONTCOUNTRY CAMPGROUND
- WILDERNESS PATROL CABIN
- FRONTCOUNTRY RANGER STATION
- FIRE LOOKOUT
- SHELTER
- —— SURFACED ROADWAY
- --- UNSURFACED ROADWAY
- PARK BOUNDARY
- TRAILS
- WONDERLAND TRAIL
- STREAMS   LAKES   GLACIERS
- •···3.7···• TRAIL DISTANCES IN MILES

WILDERNESS TRAILSIDE CAMPS

Most backpackers at Mount Rainier National Park use the trailside camps listed below. Individual sites have a capacity of five people, or one immediate family, and group sites have a capacity of twelve people.

Camping by permit is also allowed in undesignated sites within crosscountry and alpine zones throughout the park.

Camp	Indiv. Sites	Group Sites	Elev. Feet
Berkeley Park	2	1	5375
Camp Curtis	2	-	8685
Camp Muir	110*	-	10080
Camp Schurman	48*	-	9440
Carbon River	4	1	3195
Cataract Valley	6	1	4620
Deer Creek	2	-	2950
Devil's Dream	7	1	5060
Dick Creek	2	-	4185
Dick's Lake	1	-	5675
Eagle's Roost	7	-	4885
Fire Creek	3	1	4300
Forest Lake	1	-	5660
Glacier Basin	5	1	5965
Golden Lakes	5	1	5130
Granite Creek	2	1	5765
Indian Bar	4	1	5120
James Camp	3	1	4620
Klapatche Park	4	-	5515
Lake Eleanor	3	1	5000
Lake George	5	1	4320
Lower Crystal Lake	2	-	5450
Maple Creek	4	1	2815
Mystic Camp	7	1	5570
Nickel Creek	3	1	3385
N. Puyallup River	4	1	3750
Olallie Creek	2	1	3940
Paradise River	3	1	3805
Pyramid Creek	2	-	3765
Shriner Peak	2	-	5355
Snow Lake	2	-	4690
South Mowich River	4	1	2605
South Puyallup River	4	1	4000
Summerland	5	1	5940
Sunrise	8	2	6245
Tamanos Creek	4	1	5270
Three Lakes (H)	2	1	4680
Upper Crystal Lake	2	-	5825
Upper Palisades Lake	2	-	5835
Yellowstone Cliffs	2	-	5180

(H) = horse sites available

Backpacker sites are also available at the Mowich Lake and White River frontcountry campgrounds.

*Space at Camp Muir and Camp Schurman is alloted by the number of people rather than by the number of parties.

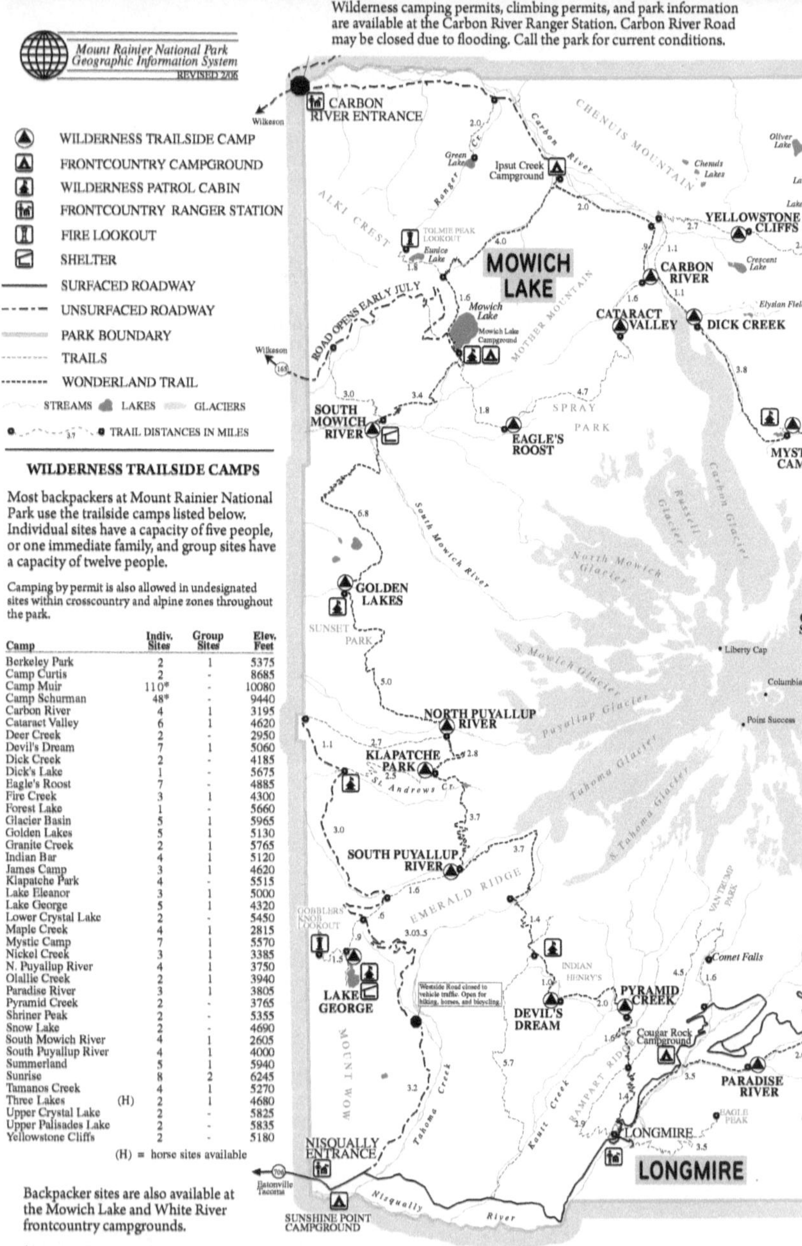

WILDERNESS TRIP PLANNER MAP

Eastside wilderness camping and climbing permits are available at the White River Wilderness Information Center in summer. In winter, permits are available at the USFS/NPS office in Enumclaw or by self-registration at the park's north entrance (SR 410 at Crystal MountainBlvd).

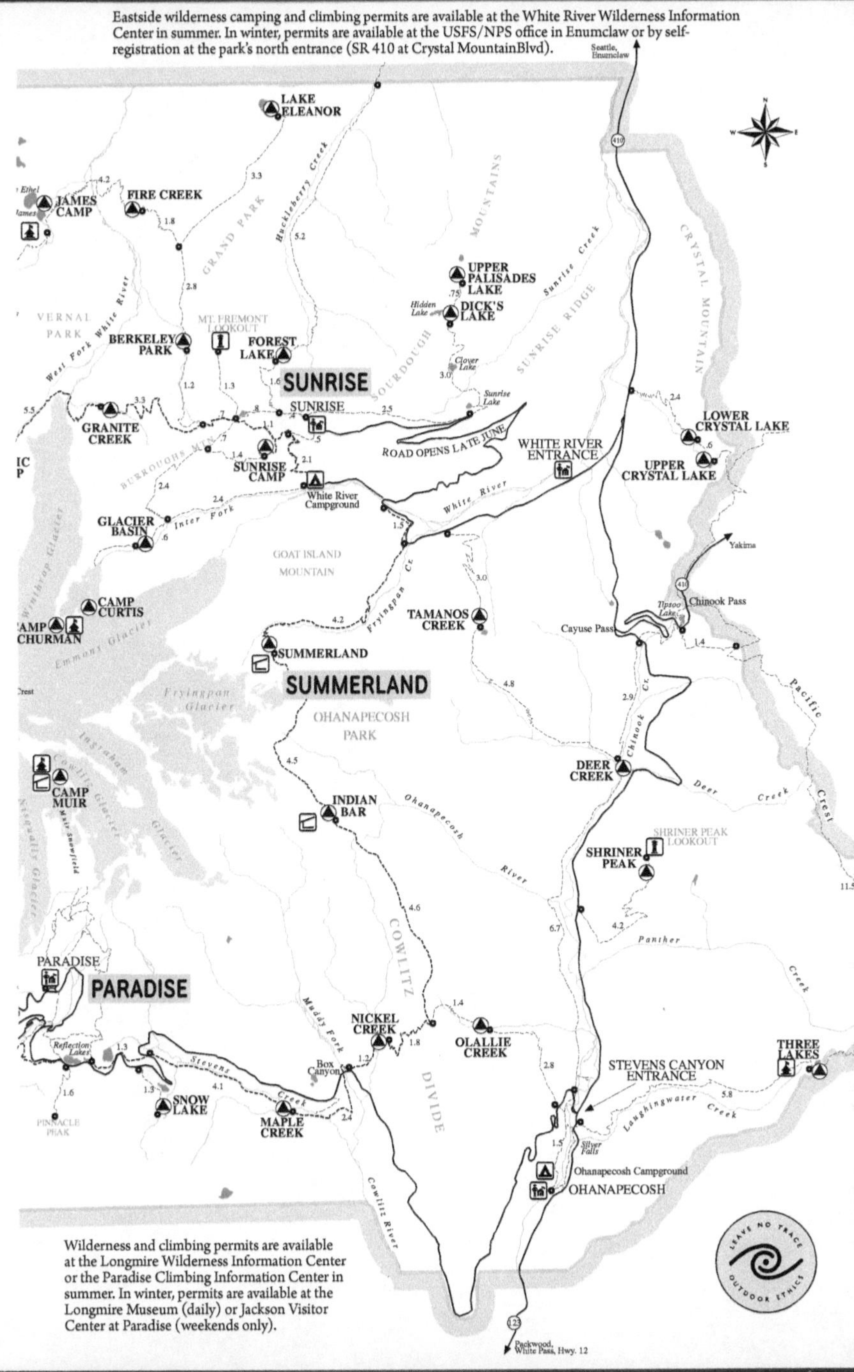

Wilderness and climbing permits are available at the Longmire Wilderness Information Center or the Paradise Climbing Information Center in summer. In winter, permits are available at the Longmire Museum (daily) or Jackson Visitor Center at Paradise (weekends only).

WONDERLAND

The mountain that was God.

— *John D. Williams*

I killed three people the year the virus came.

I woke at the Indian Bar Campground surprised to find I was still alone. When I reserved the site months ago, I was able to claim the last available spot. I expected the camp would be full for my stay but found it empty upon my arrival. No hikers had arrived in the night. There had not been another soul on the trail since the prior morning. I wondered if I was missing something. Despite hiking through one of the country's busiest national parks in the height of summer, I passed no one when I left.

Traversing to the top of Panhandle Gap, I found the snowpack heavy despite the unseasonable heat. I strapped into my microspikes to make the final climb. I was cautious, expecting the ground to turn to slush below my footfalls. The grade dropped precariously. I looked for the boot paths of those who had come through before me and tried to follow their trail. The prints were faint, plastered over with a fresh coat of snow from a recent storm.

As I crested the final peak on the Panhandle, I gazed down a boulder staircase at Fryingpan Creek and the lush meadows of Summerland below. It felt like standing on top of the world.

The sun warmed my shoulders as I picked my way down the stone steps. Water cascaded down the hillside next to me, filling my ears. I stole glances at the mountain, the peak glimpsed beyond a ridge, and listened to the marmots' whistle to each other in the distance. The meadow was ablaze with wildflowers of every color: red Indian paintbrushes, purple Alpine asters, yellow buttercups, and white avalanche lilies danced in the breeze. With Mount Rainier as the backdrop, these blossoms were the glory of Summerland. It was one of the most popular hikes in the park, and I found it deserted. It felt wrong.

I pushed the feeling to the back of my mind. There had been nothing unusual when I started the Wonderland Trail. My access point, Sunrise, sits at 6400', the highest point you can drive to on the 14410' mountain. The view from the top provides a front row seat to the glaciated volcano known as Mount Rainier and overlooks the surrounding foothills of the Cascade Mountains and distant, sister stratovolcanoes. Nine days prior, I made the drive up the long and winding road to the aerie of Yakima Park, the home of Sunrise.

On that morning, the lot was filling, but still quite empty given the early hour. I pulled into the designated area for long term parking, stepped out of my vehicle, and accessed the back hatch to pull out my backpack. A nearby group of hikers applied sunscreen despite the early hour and prepared their own packs. The threesome consisted of a woman and two men: they looked like kids, no older than their mid-twenties. They were intent on the radio, listening and speaking animatedly to each other. They were too far for me to hear the details, but I noted the look of concern on the woman's face as she glanced between her male companions. One of the men looked exasperated. I could not interpret his expression, or hers, and it distracted me from doing a thorough check of my gear. I put my head down and made a final pass over my supplies to ensure I was set to depart.

The start of my hike was uneventful. Before I began, I read several trail reports and even cruised a message board dedicated to hiking the trail. The status of all the log foot bridges, the fixtures used for crossing over rivers where permanent bridges were not possible, were all reported to be intact. It came as a relief, and while it did little to allay my fear of water crossings, I was grateful I would not need to ford the glacial tributaries. Warned beforehand, I carried extra water in the barren sections. It was a dry year. The consensus on all the websites was that it was a perfect time for the fortunate few who were able to snag a full circuit permit. I was one of the lucky ones.

Mount Rainier National Park boasts millions of visitors each year. On summer days the campgrounds are full, the trails populated, and visitor centers busy. It was not until I passed through the Devil's Dream Camp, near the halfway point, that I noticed the quiet. While not altogether abnormal, the westside section I was hiking had limited access points, the number of people I encountered was a trickle compared to the steady stream I expected. At the Pyramid Creek Campground, a pair of women occupied the only other campsite. They kept to themselves that night, which I regarded as only a little strange. I overheard their fervent whispering and assumed they were in an argument, so I gave them space. When I left the next morning, they had already gone. The following day, I crossed paths with a single man as I was leaving the Maple Creek Camp. He focused on his feet as he approached and gave me a simple nod as we passed. I had not seen anyone since.

The Wonderland trail comprises of a ninety-three-mile circuit around Mount Rainier and boasts a cumulative twenty-two-thousand feet of elevation change over that distance. It crosses glacial rivers and creeks, passes through a number of backcountry camps, and offers sights found nowhere else on Earth. It is a test of skill for even the most experienced hiker, and I was nearing the finish. A year ago, I never would have believed I could do this. The realization that only ten miles stood between me, and the completion of my hard-won journey filled me with an overwhelming sense of pride. In that moment, something expanded in my chest; a part of myself that had been dormant too long.

Mount Rainier would be my first long distance hike, a true demonstration of the skill set I had developed. If I could conquer Wonderland, I would be able to face the bigger thru-hikes I dreamed of. Someday I hoped to claim the Triple Crown of hiking: the Appalachian, Continental Divide, and Pacific Crest Trails. The thought of hiking the last on that list was what had set my heart on fire again. I did not know when I began my trip on the Wonderland that the world as I knew it would come to an end.

I wanted to stay longer in Summerland but knew my muscles

would grow cold for the last leg, so I pushed on. After descending the switchbacks below Summerland, I arrived at the faded grey log crossing the lower Fryingpan Creek. The planed edge of the log had cutwork for traction and a single shaky handrail. There was the familiar prickle of anxiety. I pushed it away, seeing the creek bed was so dry I could cross it hopping boulders. I focused myself and traversed over the bridge. On the other side, I let out the air I held. Stepping off onto the dry riverbed, I found a dirty red daypack sitting on a log. A knocked over blue water bottle lay near it on the ground. After so long without seeing anyone, I stopped and scanned the cottonwoods for signs of life. No one was there.

"Hello?" I called. No reply. Time passed, and I called again. The tipped container worried my mind, but my desire to finish the last segment of my journey urged me on. I assumed it was an impromptu bathroom break. Either they were too embarrassed to respond, or etiquette had taken them quite a distance from the creek, and they could not hear me. Despite my misgivings, I was eager to reach the end. I did not wait any longer for a response and continued on my way.

The trail passed into a close forest thick with huckleberry shrubs. I picked a few berries and tossed them into my mouth without stopping. The smell of sunlight on trees filled the air. Morning slipped into midday. This would be my last tranquil moment in the days and weeks to come, and I would reflect back to it with the hindsight only the future delivers. If I had stopped and found the hiker that owned that red backpack, would it have changed the outcome that day?

The White River is heard before it is seen. There is no mistaking its power from the approach. Mixed with the roar of the glacier water is the pounding of submerged boulders as they shift along the riverbed with the force of the flow. Ahead, the trail crossed over the river and passed into the campground of the same name. My breath quickened, and my stomach turned. Every water-crossing along the trail was difficult for me. I had hoped I would overcome it from sheer exposure, but the fear held. The bridge appeared stable, but it was a wide span over a fast current. The water churned and thrashed below.

I focused on the other side, but my mind was overwhelmed with thoughts of falling.

My heart pounded in my ears as I stepped onto the log. It was the final crossing before Sunrise. Its single handrail thrummed with the vibration of the rapidly moving water below my feet. I undid my pack's belts, feeling the entire weight of my backpack on my shoulders. It was a safety precaution. I could unshoulder the pack if I fell rather than allow it to drag me down. I clasped the rail with a sweaty palm and crossed. The river thundered in my ears. On the other side, the path was marked by logs and stones through the sand then disappeared up an embankment into dense forest. Beyond, the trail cut through the last loop of sites in a quiet campground tucked against the cliff face. I kept my head down, taking small sips of air through my nose, and watched the slow movement of each boot as I placed one in front of the other.

The edges of my vision wavered, fuzzy from the lack of oxygen. I stopped, taking a moment to inhale a lungful of air to clear my sight. I continued, unclenching only when I took cautious steps down the rock stairs on the opposite side. Despite my shaky legs, I kept moving to feel the miles continue disappearing below my feet.

As I arrived at the campground, there was only the sound of the wind through the trees. Even the birds ceased to sing. Unnerved, I blamed it on residual anxiety from the crossing. The parking lot for the picnic area was almost empty, and again, I was surprised by the lack of people. Awareness can be a slippery thing; the way your mind can slide over the things your eyes see. This discovery should have alarmed me, and yet it did not break through the threshold of my focus.

I followed the arrow down the paved road and scanned for the next sign pointing to where the trail continued. Several of the camp-sites appeared empty, but through the dense forest, tents and RVs occupied isolated sites. I expected to smell campfires or hear children playing, but White River was a ghost town. The thought was forgotten when I spotted the sign pointing to Sunrise and followed the turn to re-enter the forest. I steeled myself for the final push, fighting the exhaustion from setting in. My consciousness, grown so accustomed to deep solitude and the rhythm of my internal wilderness, focused on forward motion and lacked the presence of mind to fully grasp the setting I found myself walking through. I missed crucial details.

The climb up the final switchbacks to reach Sunrise was strenuous. Sweat drenched my back and trickled down the side of my face. I did not bother to wipe it away. I was congratulating myself for making excellent time from Indian Bar when the parking lot at the top came into view, and it became clear that something was wrong. All at once, the signs I had disregarded along the way coalesced into a whole picture.

I expected to be thrust back into a parking lot full of activity but found it empty save a few vehicles. It stopped me in my tracks. No one was hiking the meadows above. Absent were the photographers normally set up to capture Mount Rainier, the jaw-dropping titan, in all her glory. I did not see clusters of backpackers doing their final preparations before departure. The area appeared abandoned. The low-grade itch I had felt the last couple days when I noticed my solitude now became an alarm screaming red alert.

With the Sunrise Visitor Center to my left and the Day Lodge directly in front of me, I cowered behind a bushy subalpine fir and released my pack to the ground. Crouching on aching legs, I dug through the bag's front pocket in search of my car key. I could see my hatchback from here, one of few cars left in the lot. Finding the key, I zipped the pocket closed. After reconsidering, I dug out the bear spray I had stuffed to the bottom of my pack after my first night on the trail. I had nearly left it behind in the hiker box at the Mowich Campground to shed the extra weight. Bears were not as aggressive in Washington, but I kept it out of sheer caution in case I ran into any troublesome bears, or men, along the way. Now I was glad I had it. I pulled the pin on the can and placed my finger flat alongside the trigger.

I gripped the key in one hand and the bear spray in the other. I headed up the ridge and entered the lot, leaving my pack behind. Assessing the distance between me and my vehicle, I was all too aware of the open space. I forced myself into a half-jog, feeling exposed. How stupid was I being at this moment? Could there be a shooter? If so, I had made myself an easy target. Memories tried to flood in, inappropriate and unbidden. My ears rang, and goosebumps prickled across my arms despite the heat. I shook my head to rattle out the intrusive thoughts. Not now. I needed to focus on what was happening here. Why was it so empty? Where were the rangers?

With my head on a swivel and all my senses raised, I crossed cement radiating the summer sun. Despite the sticky sweat all over my body, I felt a chill run down my spine. I explained to myself this would feel silly once I drove out of here, I would see it was an emergency closure. My eyes passed over things without registering. There was an orange backpack with its contents strewn about on the ground around it. Across the lot, a car's driver-side door hung open. There was a pile of clothes crumpled on the sidewalk coming into view. Something about it made no sense, my mind recognizing its shape and not registering what it was. As I drew close, it took form like seeing a face in an optical illusion. It was a person, and they were dead. I broke into a run, and in the same instant, footsteps pounded up behind me.

I was closing in on my car when someone slammed into me. Unable to stop, I collided with the side of the car and dropped the key. The hit jarred me. For a moment, I lost all sense of what to do then remembered the bear spray in my hand. I fumbled with the trigger, aimlessly pointing it in the direction of my assailant and pulled. The spray came, but the breeze caught it, sweeping it away and grazing my own eyes and airways. An object came down on my hand, making the bones inside feel like they were fragmenting apart, and I lost the canister. It made a metallic sound as it skittered away on the concrete while I fought my watering eyes and stinging nose.

"Fuck," I cried, ducking my head into my arm to wipe my face, and saving my head from being the target of the next blow. Instead, my shoulder took the impact, flaring white-hot pain through the bone. I kept one arm over my head, shielding it blindly while pain radiated down the other. I tried to regain my equilibrium to get away. I ran into my car again, and a second strike came, the object smashing my ear. Agony erupted in my skull, the pain like a knife. A hot stream trickled down the side of my neck. I would later discover my earring had been torn out, my lobe left split and bleeding.

Rage filled me. I turned to face my assailant. Adrenaline coursed through me, igniting my instinct to fight and overriding the need to run. My attacker was a woman; petite, Asian, age undecipherable, and in her hand, she wielded a large stone. She swung it at me. I grabbed her forearm, stopping the arc before it ended in my skull. The force of my hand caused her to lose her grip on the rock, and it dropped to the concrete. My toe kicked it away as I stepped forward, leveraging her arm up over her head and forcing her backward.

"Stop!" I screamed. She was a feral animal, eyes wide and wild. Terrified. In a fever, we danced around each other, my left hand gripping her right arm at the wrist, squeezing hard as she tried to wrest it free. She was silent in response.

I was taller than her, and for a moment, believed I had the high ground until she used it against me. The little woman stepped forward, hooking her leg behind my foot, and shoved with her free hand. I fell backward, my grasp on her wrist dragging her down on top of me.

The fall knocked the wind from my lungs. In my instinct to curl into myself, I let go of her. Wheezing, I struggled to get a breath of air and failed. She used the opportunity to straddle me. This momentary lapse almost cost me my life.

Using her shins to pin my arms at the elbows, she wrapped her hands around my neck, both thumbs digging into my throat and keeping me from swallowing. There was no air. I bucked and writhed under her. Her face a mask of desperation, the little woman was strong, stronger than I could have anticipated given her small size.

Time slowed into a frozen moment. I took in her lilac fleece with the three-quarter zip, the silver metal of the zipper flashing in the sunlight. I observed the stains on the fleece, rust-colored smears. One shaped like a handprint. The vice on my throat grew tighter.

Black stars flickered at the edge of my vision. Blood on her shirt. Old blood. I had to get out of this. Using what strength I had left, I arched my hips and bucked hard. It was enough to wrench my right arm free but did little to loosen her grip on my neck. I swiped at her face with my nails, but my reach came up short. I grazed her chin, forcing her to lean away, and I managed to draw a tiny sip of air through the collapsing straw of my windpipe.

A fragment registered in my periphery. I shifted my focus there, dots clouding my vision, and saw the rock just outside of my reach. The pressure behind my eyes built like they would bulge out of their sockets. I gulped hard against her thumbnails. She gritted her teeth, a guttural sound emanating from her throat. My windpipe closed, no air. I bucked again, shoving off my left foot to grab the rock with my extended right hand. She did not foresee my plan despite how she had managed to outmaneuver me. I threw myself a second time hard to reach the stone. My nails gripped the gritty surface and rolled it into my hand.

She realized too late as I swung it hard into her skull. The mass connected with her jaw. It gave a sickening crack as something taut snapped. The hold on my throat loosened. I gasped in oxygen, my vision clearing as it flooded in. She keeled over, a slow howl escaped her gaping mouth. I was free.

Her jaw was not where it should be, her face misshapen and disfigured. I sat up and swung the stone again. It connected with her temple. She rocked back against my car with the impact, bracing herself against it. Her look changed, no longer desperate, but afraid. Pity eluded me, there was only anger now. She tried to move away but was too unsteady to gain her feet or scramble away. Her head rolled like a boxer punched one time too many. I lurched at her, full of rage. Shoving her down onto the concrete, I swung the rock again.

The woman tried to guard her head with shaking and battered hands. I forced her arms down, using the same maneuver she had used to overcome me by pinning her arms with my legs. I had hiked a hundred miles in the last nine days and a thousand before that to get here: my legs were the strongest part of my body.

I brought the stone down. A cut on her forehead opened spilling a deep red current. I hit her again. Blood sprayed from the blow. Salty droplets flicked into my mouth and blurred my vision. I did not stop. Blood splattered, obscuring her face, and covering my hands. It was slick, but I brought the rock down again. Blind with fury, putting all of my strength into each strike, I smashed it into her head over and over. I thought of nothing; both empty and consumed.

Exhaustion ended it. It collapsed upon me like a shroud. I stopped the last swing when my shoulder cramped, and I came back into myself. Clarity returned. Her head was a misshapen mass, unrecognizable and hemorrhaging. The stone in my hands was covered in her blood. I dropped it in horror, sliding away from her limp body on all fours.

The sunlight bleached all the color from my surroundings. Dizzy and sick, I scanned the area, wondering if there were others with the woman and if they were watching and waiting. Nothing had changed. My breath came out ragged. My body felt like a live wire, taut and vibrating. A bird took flight from a nearby tree, startling me with the sudden flapping of its wings.

The parking lot was eerie and empty, but the pieces were starting to make sense. Several bodies baked in the sun, and each had a milieu of flies circling. The features of each person indistinguishable beneath the writhing mass. Their bodies appeared intact from this distance. No disturbance from animals. I decided to give the corpses a wide berth. Looking closer at the remaining vehicles, the dead became evident. There were many.

Near my parked car was an SUV with a person sitting in the passenger seat, their head leaning against the window. Dried blood trailed from their eyes, nose, and ears. The SUV now serving as a tomb. A bloated body leaned against the doorway to the vault toilet. They presented similar features, blood tracks from their eyes and nose.

There was no shooter. This was something else. A virus. Scenes from different pandemic movies flashed through my mind, but it was the one with the monkey that fit. My little brother had been scared of monkeys for years after watching it. This was Ebola. I fought the gorge from rising at the sight of my blood-covered hands and ran to the water spigot. Terror rose in me. I had been exposed. I scoured my face and hands in a panic. I scrubbed the sticky blood from under my nails and soaked my hair, wishing for hot water and disinfectant. What was left of the soap in my pack was forgotten. I took off my clothes, modesty discarded, and ran them under the faucet, ringing them out until the water ran clear.

I washed off as much of the woman's blood as I could and stepped back, soaked from head to toe. My mind raced with questions. How soon would I get sick? Would it be fast? Would it be painful? My throat ached, and tears pricked my eyes. Panic began to rise inside me. On instinct, I counted backwards from five. It was a trick I learned to help me cope when my fear became overpowering. For five seconds, I would let the terror overwhelm me. I would allow myself to feel the emotion in full force, but only for five seconds.

"One," I said aloud. I cut off my tears and moved forward.

There was a way out. I searched for the key, and I found it near the woman's body. Gazing over her prone form, I surmised she must have been trapped here when it all broke down. A rush of shame went through me. I gave her a gentle nudge with my foot, a final check. Her body lolled as only the lifeless do. For several moments, I waited for her to breathe, but her chest did not rise and fall. I was afraid to touch her. Her head was a contorted mass of hair and blood. One eye swollen shut while the other watched the sky.

She was dead, and I had killed her. The act itself like a dream remembered upon waking, the filaments of memory slipping away as I struggled to grasp for them. There were blood stains on my clothes, despite my efforts to wash them. I fought the compulsion to tear them off altogether. There was no doubt of my exposure, which left my skin crawling. I imagined I could feel the pathogen infiltrating my body and blood. It was too late for that, I needed to get home. I needed to get help. I leaned over her body to unlock and open the car door. In her hand was a clump of my ash blond hair dyed red with blood. I fought my own shock and forced myself to step over her body to get into the vehicle.

"We could have helped each other," I said aloud to her and myself, "you could have told me what the hell happened before you tried to kill me." My gaze slid down. Her eye remained open, unblinking. A pit lodged in my stomach. What had I done? I slammed the door shut behind me. The air inside dense and too hot. Familiarity washed over me and, with it, safety. This space felt normal, an island in the center of the chaos. I had made it back, and now I could go home. I started the car. The radio came on blasting static. I turned down the volume, remembering how I had driven here nine days prior with the music turned up and the windows down, singing out loud, unashamed in my excitement. It seemed like another lifetime, like the memory belonged to a different person. I relaxed a little. I could drive out of here and leave this nightmare behind. I rolled down the window, which released the stale air but did little to cool the cab.

The car dinged a warning. The gas light came on. I sat stupid, confused. The tank was full before I made the drive. How could it be empty? Letting the car idle, I opened the door and hopped out, not looking at the little Asian woman. I found nothing at first glance after circling the car. Then I saw it. A small, evaporated puddle below the tank. I got on the ground, the warm concrete under my palms and strained to look under the vehicle. There was the source of the problem. A hole punched into the bottom of my tank, a crude method to extract the gas from my abandoned vehicle.

I was ready to melt down again but suppressed it. No time to lose it now, I had to go. I ran for my pack, snagging it by one strap, and dashed back, throwing it into the passenger seat through the open door. The engine continued to idle.

"Thank you, God" I muttered. I put the car into drive, and it moved forward. Even if it died, I could coast down the hill to the bottom. At least I could get off the mountain. I could try to limp the car to the highway. As I steered out of the parking lot, I put the mountain in my rearview as the sun set and cast alpenglow on Rainier's face. Relief washed over me. I would make it out of here.

My confidence was short-lived. Approaching the overlook two

miles down the road, my next problem became immediately apparent. Two cars had collided and were blocking the road down the mountain. The overlook is a natural outcropping jutting out from the hillside. The road hugged the edge of the cliffside, bending at a hairpin angle around a small parking area where people stopped to take in the views north of Rainier. I could cut through the tiny lot, but it would be tight. A short stone wall surrounded the parking area. I had one way in and one way out.

Entering would be easy from my direction of approach. There was a shoulder on this side which gave me extra space to slide my car through the gap in the wall. Once inside the lot, the difficulty would be in making the turn to exit. The maneuver required completing a sharp U-turn through the gap on the other side, which was only wide enough for a single car. I was reluctant to slow down, afraid to lose momentum, but if I took the arc too wide, I would drive off the cliff. There was no wall or guardrail to prevent my car from going over the opposite side. It was like threading a needle blindfolded, but I would have to try.

I slowed enough to make the entrance into the lot, which was the moment the car chose to gutter and die. I panicked, managing the first entrance, and aiming for the exit a couple car lengths down. There was no time to calculate the angle or my speed. I slammed on my brakes to make the turn, pulling the wheel hard to invert the direction of the car, and smashed into the corner of the wall at the edge of the lot. The airbag deployed.

Dazed for a moment, I stared at the buttons and levers around me like they were foreign objects. I got out, surveyed the damage, and tried to push my car off the wall. It took all my effort to move it back a few feet. I went to the driver-side door, bracing myself against it while trying to turn the steering wheel with my overused right arm. The wheel resisted. The car refused to budge. Without power steering, I could not turn the vehicle to make it through the gap, let alone turn it 180 degrees to face downhill. The angle was too sharp. My mind flooded with thoughts. I could walk the road and make it to the highway. It was another thirteen miles. I could flag someone down.

Would there be anyone to flag down? What kind of person would they be? I stopped.

The weight of the event, the unknown, pressed on me. I was trying to anticipate a course with no information. The airbag deflated and so did I. All the fight and fire went out of me. The tears came, and this time, I let them. I placed my head in my hands, the same hands that smashed the skull of another human being only a short time before. Despite my efforts to scrub them clean, blood was jammed under my fingernails and the deep cracks of my cuticles. What I had done to the woman disgusted me. I walked to the edge of the cliff where, in a different time, people took pictures and looked at distant mountains. I sat on the edge, dangling my feet over. My stomach flipped as I considered the valley below. The impulse came to jump. Maybe I was already dead. Those thoughts connected with something visceral. I screamed into the void, the echoes my only response.

The sky grew dark, and I watched the highway for headlights. I hoped for something, some evidence anything else existed beyond this mountain. When stars appeared and the tears stopped rolling, I climbed into the backseat of my car. Bone-weary and thirsty, I drank the last dregs of my water. I wrenched the sleeping bag free from my pack, pulled it over me, and laid down. Sleep came fast.

Knocking woke me. Through closed lids, I could see the faint glow of pre-dawn and struggled to recall where I was. My heart pounded, an adrenaline punch from being startled awake. I opened my eyes, surprised to find myself in the back seat of my car. It was quiet. Had I dreamt the knocking? I sat up to overlook a panorama of hills sprawling away for miles against an indigo sky. The prior day flooded back. The knocking came again. The woman stood at the window, the one I had killed.

I screamed and scuttled away, slamming into the opposite door. Blood stained her lilac fleece. It dripped down the side of her face out of her mangled head. From her bulging left eye, she watched me for a moment then laughed. She had been dead. I had seen it for myself. How could she be alive? How could anyone survive that?

I looked around for a weapon, locating a flashlight on the floorboard. I grabbed it and exited out the door at my back, putting the car between us. My head throbbed. She had turned away to take in the changing colors of early morning. She glanced back at me over her shoulder. A fresh droplet of blood streaked down her cheek. I considered the possibility of zombies and dismissed it when she spoke.

"Su-Jin," she said, pointing a finger at herself.

"What?"

She touched her chest. "I am Su-Jin."

We stared at each other for a moment. I contemplated throwing the flashlight at her.

"Don't throw that at me," she said. Her expression flat.

"How are you here?" I asked.

"I'm here." She shrugged.

"That's doesn't answer my question. Am I dreaming this?" It was a stupid thing to say. She laughed then sauntered back in the direction I had fled from the day prior. From Sunrise.

"So, you tried to kill me. You're injured, and now, we are supposed to be friends?" I called after her. She gave no reply.

"Do you need my help?" I tried. She continued to walk. My patience already thin, I took several long strides and tried to grab her. My hand passed through her arm. She turned and looked at me with a surprised face. I recoiled, my hand tingling. Her exaggerated expression made my stomach turn, the eye grotesque up close.

"Oh? You going to kill me again?" she sneered through her words. I drew back, staring at my hands.

"Am I dead?" I asked.

"I wish," she said. We stared at each other.

"I killed you."

"Yes."

"How are you here?" I asked. She continued to stare at me, mute, then turned on her heel and walked away. *This is what it feels like to lose your mind,* I thought. I decided she was a hallucination, something my mind was offering up. As if I needed this experience to be any more difficult, now I was going crazy. I shook my head, trying to straighten myself out.

Walking back to the car, I opened the trunk and pulled out a couple of bottles of water I had stored for emergencies. They were lukewarm. I drank half of one then pulled out my pack, located my stove, and set about making a cup of coffee. I sat down on the concrete with my legs splayed before me, leaning up against the same stone wall that had left me stranded in this spot. As I waited for the water to boil, I inventoried my food supply. I was ravenous, but I did not know where my next source would be.

I did not have much left: a couple protein bars, half a bag of jerky, two energy gels, and a few packets of instant coffees. I congratulated myself on the preparation and knew it would not last long. I tore open a protein bar with my teeth and wolfed down half in one bite.

The water bubbled, I poured the instant coffee into the pot, swirling it around, and set it aside to cool. It seemed I had a companion. A dead one.

I looked up the hill after Su-Jin. She stood by the cement wall, looking out over the hills away from me. In profile her injuries were hidden, and she looked like any middle-aged Asian woman contemplating the morning, until she turned. The wound of her dashed skull reminded me of a macabre Halloween mask. The food in my mouth formed a dry lump I was unable to choke down. With a burning swig of coffee, I swallowed, and my swollen throat resisted. I wrapped the remainder of the protein bar for later.

I scanned the sky for planes, knowing the surrounding mountains were below a flight path with regular air traffic. I watched the sky as I drank my coffee, careful to blow on each sip. I focused on a couple of fading stars, searching for a blinking light or motion to suggest flight. Not a single plane crossed overhead or in the distance.

The final pull of coffee almost did not go down, my esophagus inflamed from strangulation. Without a mirror to do a full inspection, I used my hands to do a quick check of my body. I felt the lump on my shoulder where the woman had smashed the stone meant for my skull. It was sensitive to the touch. Both arms had bruises deep in the muscle tissue where she had pinned me. My right arm ached from overuse. My elbows were grated raw from rubbing against concrete and a collection of tiny scabs dotted the skin and caught the threads of my shirt. My ear lobe hung, separated. I winced when I touched it, carefully feeling the tender shreds where the earring had been ripped out. I wondered again how long it would take for symptoms to show up. How would I tell if I was sick? My body was sore from both the hike and the fight, would I even know? I continued to monitor the sky.

"It didn't matter anyway," I said out loud, "someone siphoned all my gas. There's a big hole in the bottom of the tank." I did not glance up to see if she heard me. I could feel her standing there in her stupid, stained fleece with her disgusting face.

I had the urge to hurl more insults at her but bit my tongue. Anger was coming out. I was the one trapped here now, and I did not even know why. I nursed my resentment, allowing it to grow. *Why not just ask for help?* I thought. Shame gnawed at my subconscious. I tried to push it from my mind, but my thoughts kept dragging me back to the memory of how the rock felt dislocating her jaw. It made me shudder. To distract myself, I got busy storing away the food and sleeping bag then lifted the pack onto my protesting shoulders.

I decided to abandon the car. It would be here if I needed it. I would head back to Sunrise to find food and supplies. There had to be something there I could use. When Su-Jin saw me coming toward her, she walked ahead of me down the middle of the road. Her head continued to ooze blood like a dripping faucet. I avoided looking at her as we marched up the hill in silence. The peak of Mount Rainier came into view. I stored a disconcerting realization in the back of my mind: not a single airplane had crossed the sky.

The two miles back to Sunrise took less than an hour. Su-Jin stayed in front of me and did not look back. I re-entered the lot uneasy, scanning for a second attacker. Su-Jin's remains were scattered across the asphalt, spread out from where I had left her the day before. A large animal had been here. A murder of crows picked at what was left. The birds did not land on the remaining corpses. It gave me pause. I checked on Su-Jin walking ahead of me, thinking she did not notice the tableau.

"I wasn't sick," she called back to me, as if reading my mind. "Animal don't eat the sick."

I went to the water faucet first and filled my water bottle then headed into the ranger station. I drank as I walked, the cold water helping alleviate my sore throat. When I reached the door, it was a relief to find it unlocked. The old building was dark with wood-paneled walls and hardwood floors. I tried the switch, and the lights came on. I suspected solar power ran the building. I found no bodies inside.

The room held two desks littered with the usual detritus of office supplies and bits of paper. A large map of the park and surrounding national forests dominated one wall, and there were shelves full of literature and pamphlets around the room. I wondered how long ago the station had been abandoned. On one of the desks sat a full cup of coffee like someone had walked away from it without taking a sip. The room frozen in a moment like a snapshot.

I did not know what I was looking for. I scanned the desktops for reports or news but found only official park documents and scribbled notes. I had hoped for an explanation about a park closure or a bulletin about a virus.

Upon emerging from the building, a breeze picked up and blew in the fetid smell of decay. I felt my gorge rise. I had to get out of here, but first, needed to replenish my stores. I hoped caches remained. To reduce weight while backpacking Wonderland, hikers had the option to store caches containing three to four days' worth of food at designated locations around the mountain. If my gas tank was any indicator, I had no reason to be optimistic. In Sunrise, the cache buckets were stored at the old gas station, a remnant of a time when commercial enterprise had a presence in Mount Rainier. Today it served as a historical artifact and a checkpoint for Wonderland hikers.

When I opened it, several buckets were stacked inside. No one else had thought to check here. Each displayed a name and a number along with the date of pick up, each representing a person who never collected it. I opened the oldest first since it was several days past its intended pick-up.

Every bucket is like a time capsule, full of treasures from a different life. A life where the world did not collapse. A life filled with the anticipation of a completed journey. I wondered who they were. How old was Shannon? What was she like? I tried to decipher their personalities based on their brands and preferences. I guessed their special items. People often packed treats for their food pick-up, heavy items or things that would take up too much space in their backpacks. Shannon had left herself a bottle of Snoqualmie root beer. The bottle retained the cold from the prior night. I opened and drank it without guilt. The contents seared my throat, but I ignored it, letting out a satisfying belch of foam when I finished.

Shannon and I could have been friends. We shared the same taste. Along with standard items like protein bars and cajun-style trail mix, she included a bag of dried cinnamon apples, packets of spicy tuna and chicken salad, a pouch of peanut butter, Landjägers, and tortillas. There were several freeze-dried meals: all beef stroganoff. Finding them almost made me laugh out loud. Beef stroganoff was my favorite.

My last food cache had been in Longmire three days prior. Heavy rainfall had woken me early. I was unable to sneak in any more sleep despite my fatigue, so I strapped on my headlamp and gathered my tent. I noted the two women had left in the night and concluded it was due to the rain. I lamented having to pack the soaked tent away, knowing I would have to dry everything out the first chance I had to keep it from smelling. I opted for an energy gel rather than boil water for coffee in a downpour. Before I even got back on the trail, I was despondent, tired, and soaked, with only my feet saved thanks to my waterproof boots. My rain jacket, on the other hand, seemed to function better as a greenhouse, trapping the moist Washington air underneath it rather than keeping it out.

It had been an early weekday morning, dawn on the cusp of breaking when I reached Longmire. I arrived in the middle of a downpour, the kind where the water fell with such ferocity, I kept my hood pulled down over my head to keep the rain from running into my eyes. Fog hung at the tips of all the trees, and every plant glistened with moisture. Rainstorms were common here, even in the height of summer. It was a well-known fact the mountain created her own atmosphere, and today, the entire park appeared to be under a low-hanging weather system that showed no signs of relenting.

Longmire received the highest number of visitors in Mount Rainier. It was open year-round and gave access to many of the most popular hikes and views in the park. People visited the store and restaurant or stayed at the inn. Even in the early hours, a flow of cars arrived each day, passing through to drive to Paradise to catch the first morning light on the mountain. The emptiness had not occurred to me as strange. In truth, I had given little notice to the quiet road or the lack of people due to the early hour and terrible weather.

When I walked into Longmire on that morning, I could not see past my own misery. I huddled under an eave next to the Wilderness Information Center and stuffed the food from my cache into my bag. I did not bother with the treats I had packed. Already drenched with miles to cover, I moved on to the Maple Creek Campground with the hope of a break in the weather. The restaurant was closed, and it would be hours until it would open, so there was no reason to stay despite planning to sit down to a full breakfast.

Did I remember cars passing through or was I too much in my head to notice? I remembered it being the worst day on the trail. The additional weight of the water soaking my pack and clothing had slowed me down. When I arrived at Maple Creek, it had been empty and had remained empty during my stay. I assumed the weather had deterred others from camping, and although it was odd given the season, I chose to disregard it as unusual. Perhaps that had been a mistake.

Setting aside Shannon's cache, I opened the next which contained similar items, but different brands and flavors. It boiled down to the same essential meals. I guessed they were vegetarian given the absence of animal protein. The treat in the third was a bag of chocolate peanut butter candies. The next contained a jalapeno cheese dip and tortilla chips. I imagined making nachos which made me smile. I packed my bag with as much as I could carry and decided to move the rest into the station for safe keeping. If Su-Jin survived, it was still possible there would be others.

I rounded the corner carrying a bucket in each arm to find Su-Jin surveying the lot.

"It happened fast," she said, a sad look on the side of her face still able to make expressions. "Now all dead."

"What happened?" I demanded, grasping at the first bit of information. She glared at me and clucked in a language I did not understand. I rolled my eyes and walked past her.

"Casper the unhelpful ghost," I muttered. After stashing the remaining food in the station's closet, I scanned the room for anything useful. Nothing stood out.

After a bit of searching, I found a ring of keys in the top drawer of the desk with the abandoned mug of coffee on it. I located the one I needed and locked the closet door. I yanked on the handle to confirm it latched, holding the ring secure in my hand.

My mind flashed to losing the key, being strangled, the blood-covered stone. I almost dropped the ring, but managed to jam it into my pocket, the sick twist of shame in my gut. I glanced up at Su-Jin standing outside the door. She continued to look out into the parking lot at her own body. My eyes welled. I counted backward from five and shrugged it away. There were things I needed to do.

The Visitor Center was prominent at the far end of the parking lot. I was drawn to it, wondering what I might find inside. Approaching the door, the interior was cast in morning light through the curtain walling. The door resisted as I braced it open. The Center was constructed like an old log cabin with a vaulted ceiling, creating an open airy space. There was a three-dimensional topographic map of Mount Rainier on one side of the room and an enormous fireplace filling the wall on the other. Benches and wooden rocking chairs surrounded the hearth as a communal area. The room smelled of old woodsmoke and corruption.

In the center of the room were various display cases detailing the eruption path of the volcano, preservation of the Sunrise area, and in-depth information about the local flora and fauna. Framed sepia-colored photographs hung from the walls describing the history of the area. As I moved around a display, a man came into view. He sat in a rocking chair in front of the cold fireplace, the ashes of the fire still at his feet. Dried streaks of blood leaked from his eyes and blotted his skin. I pulled a handkerchief from my pack and tied it around my face. The smell was overwhelming. For one horrid moment, I thought he might reanimate. Unsettled by his presence, I watched him out of the corner of my eye.

There was a small camp store tucked beside the ranger's desk with a collection of items for both tourists and hikers. Here you could buy clothes, books, and posters. The store also maintained an odd sampling of backpacking gear. Clothes yanked from hangers lay on the floor amongst the glass from the shattered case. I stepped over the mess, fragments of glass crunching beneath my boots. I scanned to see what I could use. From the case, I grabbed several fuel canisters, a small hatchet, and a backup water bladder. I took one last look around the room, a final glance at the dead man, and slipped out.

The Sunrise Snack Bar occupied the main area of the Day Lodge, accessed through a side door around the corner from the ranger station. From this angle I could see it was dark inside. I was reluctant to go inside, feeling the day begin to slip away from me, but felt compelled to do a quick investigation. I crossed the lot, Su-Jin trailing behind. When I drew closer, I saw one of the doors braced open by a large stone. A sharp stab of fear shot through my chest. I would not be caught off guard again. I loosened the hatchet from my pack.

The interior was cast in shadows. I picked up a pebble and tossed it inside, hoping to startle any animals, or people, that might be inside. Silence was the only response. I took a slow step in, allowing my eyes to adjust to the darkness. The menu on the back of the wall advertised an elk burger for fifteen dollars and a side of fries for five dollars more.

The chairs were turned upside down on the tables, counters wiped down and clean, like any ordinary morning.

My ears attuned to a faint hum coming from the kitchen, one I recognized as a refrigerator. Power was running to the building, but the lights did not work when I tried the switch. Once I became aware of it, the sound overwhelmed me. It was eerie against the silence and grew from faint to deafening, flooding my senses. I had gathered what I needed for now, so I exited into the bright sunlit morning.

On the sidewalk, I emptied and reorganized my pack to fit my new supplies and replenished food with my gear. It was a relief to have food and know where to get more. I would not starve. I planned to check the rest of the café another time. I pulled out the remaining half of protein bar I carried and forced it down.

The minutes were passing, and I intended to make camp before nightfall. Sunrise had easy access to supplies and existing structures. Now that I had the hatchet, I could defend myself against an attacker. And yet, the empty lot unsettled me. I felt exposed because of the road and many intersecting trails. I was afraid. On the earlier hike up, I had considered my options and found no resolution. I felt myself resisting a stay in Sunrise, talking myself out of it at every turn. My encounter with Su-Jin had made a lasting impression. I wanted to get away from places where people might go, which ruled out the nearby White River Campground as well.

My mind returned to Summerland. There was an old and well-built stone shelter there. The camp buttressed a cliff face overlooking Fryingpan Creek and Panhandle Gap. The shelter guarded against weather except for one open wall where the wind could reach in. Trees helped form a barrier along the cliff face. It would make a fine temporary home while I formulated a better plan. Summerland was a five-mile hike from the nearest road, making it difficult to access, and offered little to unwanted visitors. The major downfall to making camp there was the distance to my supply cache, and I could only carry so much. It came down to either getting over the fear or getting comfortable making the journey, and right now, the fear monster was winning. Fatigue wore at my muscles, but my mind was in overdrive, both hyper-alert and stretched too thin. I drank half of my water sensing my dehydration. It helped to clear the mental fog. What I needed now was rest.

I filled my water bottle one last time, soaking my kerchief and tying it around my neck, and stored the water bladder as a precaution. After tightening my shoelaces and adjusting the straps on my pack, I left Sunrise behind. I cut down the Sunrise Rim Trail to meet up with the Wonderland. It would be close to eleven miles before I reached my destination. I tried not to think too hard about the distance. I picked my way down the trail, gentle at first, then braced against the steady downward slope.

I anticipated sitting down to a big meal and sleeping for as long as I wanted. I had no idea what would come after. The future had become a blank space. My brain wanted to examine what had transpired while I had been hiking Wonderland but realized I had so little information, it was a fruitless and speculative venture. Were there other survivors? Was it limited to this area? Was help coming? A part of me grasped onto the possibility, a glimmer of hope, but on a deeper level, I did not believe anyone was coming. If they did, it would not be to help.

It brought me a measure of comfort to focus on what I had. I mentally ticked off all the gear I carried, what I had inventoried and stored at Sunrise, and what more I could source from other locations, abandoned vehicles, RVs and buildings. Natural endorphins flooded my system as my body fell into motion. I relaxed and felt a small shred of gratitude that, at least, I was prepared to endure.

Lost in thought when I reached the White River Campground, I slowed to look around. It was surprising to see again with fresh eyes and new awareness. How could I have missed what seemed so obvious now? Vehicles sat. Whole campsites had been abandoned, and tents stood with rain flies rippling in the cool breeze that flowed through the canyon. Stoves were set up on picnic tables. Knocked over camp chairs laid in the dirt. Animals had been at the coolers, and the squirrels were quarreling over the scraps.

A camper sat with its door hanging open. I hesitated, the urge to check, but did not dare a closer inspection. I already guessed what I would find. For a moment, I considered exploring the campground, seeing the potential for supplies everywhere. Between my desire to reach Summerland and the lack of room in my bag, I dismissed the idea outright. There was another holding area for food caches here, and I made a mental note of the potential resource. As I passed through the campground, the sound of the river grew, echoing throughout the canyon. Dread welled inside me.

Full body fatigue was taking over, my pack heavier today than the entirety of my Wonderland circuit. Sleeping in the backseat of my car had left a painful knot in my thigh. I decided to take a break before crossing to stretch it out and sat down on a boulder by the river's edge.

Growing up, I had spent a lot of time in the lowlands along this river, skipping rocks across its smoother sections or lying in the grass near its edge. My friends and I used to explore the woods surrounding the tributary, uncovering nooks where older kids partied and planning forts to build. On hot days, we walked out on the narrow deltas of rocks and sand and watched the tiny salmon spawn languish in the slow offshoots of the river. I remembered that girl, the fearless one. The younger version of me, the one that existed before life changed, had plunged into this river at thirteen. Lithe in a bikini, tanned from long summer days, my friends dared me to jump in. I accepted, unafraid, and executed a perfect cannonball into the icy glacial waters.

In hindsight, it was a dangerous and reckless thing to do. First, I was not a strong swimmer and never had been, despite years of lessons at the local community pool. Second, the White River was colloquially known as the Stuck for good reason. Its waters were muddy and grey from runoff and riddled with debris and downed trees collected from as far as the Emmons Glacier, where the White River originated.

Not knowing the hazards hidden in the water, I launched myself off the concrete block of the fish ladders, hurtling midair in the sweet release of flight to collide with the shocking blast of near freezing water. My breath was torn from my lungs, and yet, I felt no fear. On instinct, I made my body long, allowing the roiling current to carry me downstream instead of fighting against it. I bounced off erosion smoothed boulders and received a gash in my thigh from an unseen branch. When I climbed out, my friends cheered my bravery. My older self regarded that moment as one of pure stupidity and smiled.

In the present, I channeled the brave one, my younger self, to cross the river. That girl of thirteen; the one blissfully unaware of what suffering was to come in her life. I stepped onto the bridge. Taking careful, determined steps, I skimmed my hand along the rail until I reached the other side. I allowed myself a moment of fulfillment. After so long, it felt like progress.

With the crossing behind me, I re-entered the forest and pressed on. Birds cast their voices as echoes among the tall redwood trees. I had lost Su-Jin before the campground, and I was unconcerned.

I tuned in to my primitive senses; monitoring my breathing and the condition of my body, focusing on the performance of each of my muscles as they carried me along. The physical demand being simple and uncomplicated. The state of walking alone in the woods is akin to a deep meditation. With each step, I grounded myself in presence and ultimate awareness.

The rhythm of my footfalls on the path lulled me into something like a trance. I observed my mind from the outside, and my thoughts became focused and reflective. I noticed the raindrops on a leaf and how light refracted through each droplet like a tiny crystal. I heard the squish of mud beneath my boot, that tactile connection to the earth. The moments, fleeting and temporary in their existence: a tiny grey mushroom hiding beneath a fallen redwood, a watchful squirrel flicking his tail with interest, the rays of light shining through the trees and shimmering through the mist. We travelers live for these encounters because they are a true spiritual experience.

Deep in the forest, the world comes back to me with a scent: the sweet mixture of huckleberries and sun-warmed pine needles. The aroma cut through my empty thoughts and awoke a raw hunger. I dropped my pack, the fuel canisters clanging together inside the bag and waded into the shrubs. Dew covered huckleberries of deep purple surrounded me in every direction. I popped a couple in my mouth, their tang making my jaw ache. Once started, I could not stop. I tossed berries into my mouth as fast as I could pick them. Their flavor was marvelous. I ate them in a sort of frenzy, gathering handfuls at a time and shoving them into my mouth until my cheeks bulged, chewing while I gathered more. I felt each burst upon my tongue with their sweet juice. My stomach welcomed the sugar, grateful for sustenance.

As I reached for another branch to pull toward me, I caught a glimpse of my fingers soaked in the huckleberry juice, a deep red. A wave of nausea came over me. Su-Jin jumped up in front of me. Her mangled wounds fresh, spilling crimson blood matching my fingertips. She pursed her lips and laughed.

"Stupid asshole, you forgot about me," she said, rage burning in her eyes. I turned away and fought my rising gorge. My legs shook trying to maintain purchase on the hillside covered in loose tree duff and soft earth. My body resisted the impulse to retch, holding back the food to fuel my overworked and underfed muscles. It was strange to both want to expel the berries in my belly and feel my body fight against the evacuation. I hunched over, taking slow, deep breaths of air through my nose. Gagging once, my mouth salivated in preparation to vomit.

Su-Jin chortled, pleased with herself, and waded out of the patch. I followed, grabbing my water bottle, and taking tiny sips of lukewarm water. The hunger was gone. I felt sure I would never want huckleberries again as they sat uncomfortably in my stomach. The queasiness passed, albeit slowly, and I felt better. Su-Jin walked up the trail ahead of me, not bothering to wait. This section was a comfortable leg, flat and wide, with few roots or stones on the path. It was a relief given the growing exhaustion I felt. The sugar from the berries I did consume would help me up the final switchbacks to the camp.

We arrived at the Fryingpan crossing. The backpack from the day before remained. An ominous warning now. A red flag missed. Only twenty-four hours had passed, and it felt like the longest day of my life. I took my pack off to move further into the shrubs. Without the weight of the bag, I felt as if I was defying gravity balancing from rock to rock.

Behind a small cluster of young cottonwoods, I found the pack's owner. A young man, wearing black basketball shorts and a t-shirt cut off at the arms, slumped against a boulder. His complexion was dark and like the others, dried blood crusted from his nose and ears. I drew closer and saw deep purple, almost black, bruising on his arms and legs. He smelled of death, an odor I was becoming familiar with. I pulled my damp handkerchief over my face from where I had left it tied around my neck. Animals had not disturbed his body, and gauging by how bloated he was, I suspected he had died a few days ago. I had an impulse to move him out of the riverbed and cover him.

"Don't," Su-Jin said, peering out from behind the brush. "Don't touch him." With that, she disappeared into the foliage. I stood there alone with the corpse. I took one last look, wondering what brought him to this place, then followed Su-Jin.

The switchbacks felt unending. Every landing was an opportunity to stop and catch my breath. It took all my will to drag my feet up the last two sections, both my calves burning with every step. Reaching the top, I crossed the alpine meadow in the late afternoon heat. Rainier filled the western horizon. The marmots' playground quiet and abandoned. The wildflowers shimmied and shook in the gentle breeze. Relief washed over me walking up the final slope to the campground. There was no sound on the air except the distant cascading water of the creek. The group shelter was empty. I dropped my bag inside the old stone building then took a slow painful walk through the other campsites, four in total, to verify my solitude. I was alone.

To see Summerland, empty at the height of the season, was unsettling. I set up my tent inside the shelter, rolled out my air mattress, and waited for it to fill. I tossed my sleeping bag on top and forced a couple of breaths into my pillow. I wanted to lie down at that moment, but instead, made myself leave the shelter one last time to collect water, having emptied the contents of my bottle during the hike. Before settling in, I prepared a packet of beef stroganoff. After managing to eat half, I grew sleepy, so I resealed the bag and lay down on my sack. Within seconds, my mind swam, and I was gone.

I woke after sundown with the fading remnants of daylight still warming the sky and casting growing shadows. What had woken me was unclear. Suspecting the fullness of my bladder to be the culprit, I resisted the familiar pressure. My feet ached and felt swollen in their socks, my neck was stiff from my underinflated pillow. My shoulder throbbed, flaring in protest when I rolled onto it by mistake. A mosquito's tinny, high buzzing hovered near my head.

My tent door hung open. I sighed, rebuking myself for falling asleep without shutting it. My body felt like it was trapped in cement, unable to move. But something had pierced through my unconsciousness. I fought against the fog of sleep. My eyes adjusted to the low light, and I saw Su-Jin standing on the cliff edge looking outward through the trees toward Panhandle Gap, the damage to her face in shadow.

"Someone's coming," she whispered.

The electric jolt of panic ran through me, forcing me up. I went to empty my bladder first. Tight muscles restricted my movement, leaving me stiff and moving like a marionette. My head swam, unfocused from interrupted sleep and overcome with heart-pounding adrenaline. I grabbed my water bottle to wash away the dry sandpaper from my mouth then made my way over to where Su-Jin stood.

Amongst the boulders, a small headlamp bounced and bobbed in the darkness as its invisible owner picked their way down the trail. Someone was coming. I marked their speed, their progress slow as they attempted to navigate the stone stairs without the benefit of full light. In daylight, it was treacherous on tired legs, one toe catch and you got a face full of volcanic rock.

I had to act fast but found it hard to gather my muddy thoughts. I returned to the shelter in the dark, found my headlamp after a quick search, and put it around my head, leaving it off for fear of alerting the stranger. I loosened the hatchet from my pack, feeling its sharp edge with the tips of my fingers, and returned to the cliff side where I watched the beam float along and enter the valley.

They approached without sound and moved forward without looking back or slowing to guide the way. I felt confident, whoever it was, they were alone. My heart hammered in my chest so hard it was difficult to breathe. The fear threatened to eat me alive. I was not ready for another confrontation. Su-Jin watched me from her place by the cliffside.

"You going to kill this one too?" she said, unamused. I ignored her. She reverted to her native tongue again, nattering at me. Her voice grated on my threadbare nerves. The light disappeared as it followed the trail behind a grove of trees. I moved into the darkness of the shelter, placing the walls behind me to prevent being surprised. I was backing myself into a corner, but I would not allow someone to get the jump on me again. I heard the faint rustle of cautious footsteps coming up the path. They stopped at the edge of the clearing. I squinted at the brightness of his light.

"Hello?" A male voice called.

With hatchet in hand, I waited in the gloom of the shelter, silent. He came further into the camp, walking up to Su-Jin so close she could touch him. She stared into his face, unseen. His light illuminated her features, and yet he passed over her like she was nothing more than air. His features lacked distinction in the shadow of his headlamp. He was thin and the creases on his face suggested his age. He had a bandana around his head to hold back his long hair. He turned to shine the beam into the shelter.

He yelped when he saw me, grabbing his chest. He took in my weapon and changed his stance, lifting his hands above his head.

"Hi. I wasn't sure anyone else would be here," he said.

I said nothing in response but turned my lamp on. He rocked from foot to foot, casting nervous glances at the hatchet. He looked around to the other camps.

"Is it just us?" he asked, disbelief in his voice. For a second, I considered lying. He might be gauging if he could overpower me. If I was alone, he could take everything and leave me for dead. I hesitated because I saw something else in his eyes: shock, confusion, all the things I had felt in the last day and a half. He was asking out of hope that we were not alone. My guard came down a little.

"Just me," I replied. He rested his palms on the top of his head. A flash from his headlamp blinded me, and I took a step back against the wall, raising my weapon on reflex.

"Oh, I'm sorry," he apologized, sounding alarmed and distressed. He fumbled with his light and pointed it to the ground. "I was hiking the trail, and something happened. Everyone is gone. I can hardly believe what I saw in Longmire." He grew quiet. I lowered the hatchet but kept it ready.

He lowered his hands to his sides. His shoulders slumped. The man was exhausted. He unclipped his pack and lowered it to the ground, taking his water bottle from the side pocket, then sat on top of the pack, hanging his head. It was easy to see he was here for the same reason I was. This man reflected my experience, my fatigue. My concern eased further.

"It wasn't just Longmire," I replied. He continued like he had not heard me.

"It was a nightmare. There were so many dead bodies. I haven't seen anyone on the trail since. I stayed in the backwoods when I reached the campground at Cougar Rock. More bodies, sick people— I pushed to make it here. I had a feeling if anyone was left, they would be here, and I was right." He gave a faint smile. His voice grew thick and choked, "I am so glad to see you. I'm sorry I scared you."

This man must have been desperate, or crazy, to cross Panhandle Gap in full darkness with only his headlamp to guide him. The ground treacherous in the best of circumstances, I could not imagine what he had seen that chased him over it. His anguish seemed genuine, but I remained guarded.

His stifled sobs lasted only a moment before settling into quiet sniffles. He cleared his throat, embarrassed. I looked on as he regained his composure. I recognized how he suppressed his emotions as they became overwhelming. The behavior was familiar to me, a pattern I executed often enough it helped me understand something fundamental about this man's inner world.

"What's your name?" I asked.

"Ford," he replied with more throat clearing punctuated by a drink of water. "Nice to meet you." He said the last bit out of habit, not considering the circumstances were far from nice. He made no attempt to stand or shake my hand, remaining seated on his bag in a defensive position. I wanted to believe him.

"Are you sick?" he asked. The question caught me off guard, although it was an obvious one. More than twenty-four hours had passed since my altercation with Su-Jin. It had not occurred to me I had no symptoms. Fatigue and battle wounds aside, the virus had passed over me. In Ford's case, it appeared to have missed him too.

"I don't think so," I replied.

"I don't think I am either," he responded, "but I am not certain I would know for sure. It seems to happen fast, but I guess incubation—" He trailed off rather than give in to idle speculation and looked pained.

I thought of the bodies at Sunrise. The blood from the eyes, nose, and ears. I wondered how bad it was in Longmire. If it was worse than Sunrise, and I suspected it was, then I could understand Ford's need to get away from there as fast as possible. I relaxed my grip on the weapon, my palm sweating against the wooden handle, but I did not put it down.

"I'm Peri. I finished Wonderland a couple days ago in Sunrise. No one was left alive. I don't know what's going on. I looked for information but couldn't find anything." The words were a half-truth. I felt a pang in my stomach when I spoke the word 'alive', a casual lie. The weight of Su-Jin's gaze pressed on me.

Ford gave a deep sigh. It did not seem possible for his shoulders to sink any lower and yet somehow, they did. The look of utter defeat.

"It wasn't just Longmire, then. I knew it was too hopeful to think it was isolated. I heard something about this before I hit the trail, but I guess we all underestimated the reports," he said.

"What reports?" I asked. He looked up at me.

"I heard on the news that some cases of Ebola were showing up in Portland. Some environmental group released it," he responded.

"Someone did this? Why?" I asked. I latched on to the single piece of information.

"Honestly? I don't know. The only thing I know about the group, Mother something— I can't remember their name, was that they would set themselves on fire on the steps of the Supreme Court. They were fanatical about global warming. The news outlets have been ignoring them for years, at least until they were connected to this. Every so-called pandemic they warn about: Swine Flu, SARS, Coronavirus. It seems like nothing much happens, so I didn't take this too seriously either. Last I heard, they were containing it. I figured it would blow over." He stared off after finishing his sentence, looking troubled. I considered his words.

"Beyond that, I can only speculate. As much as I would love to continue conversing with you, I can barely think straight. I am going to set my tent up on that ridge." He pointed up the hill. "I was supposed to stop at Paradise River late yesterday but kept moving. I slept off trail but not for very long. Can we talk more tomorrow?" He stood up, lifted his pack by one strap and waited for a reply before he moved.

"Okay," I answered, not knowing what else to say. He began to trudge away then stopped.

"You have every reason to be worried about me. You are smart to be fearful, but I am safe. I have no way to prove it, but I promise you are safe. I will keep my distance. You won't see me in the morning unless you want to, but I will say: I am glad to see you. I was afraid I would be alone."

I said nothing else but waited for him to make his way up the hill. Once I heard the rattle of tent poles, I relaxed a little. I allowed some time to pass then crawled back into my tent. The hatchet remained by my side, my hand resting on it while I lay awake listening to the wind tangle through the branches above the shelter. I thought about what he had said about the environmental group and searched my own memory. I came up empty. Sometime in the night Su-Jin began to sing a low, quiet song. Her voice was haunting and beautiful. It carried me away.

The sun was several hours above the horizon, the birds long past morning song, when I woke. My body gave vicious protest when I moved. Sweat covered my body, the summer heat already in full swing. I forced myself up to gather water and empty my bladder, both necessities. My leg muscles ached on the short walk to the Fryingpan where I filtered creek water into my bottle. I thought of the young man in the dry riverbed downstream. Drinking the crisp water invigorated me and cleared my fatigue-ridden mind. I filtered more and returned to my tent, my legs loosening from the movement and hydration.

Any fear I might have had about Ford was unfounded. He kept his promise and stayed out of sight. Collecting a couple of oatmeal packets, some dried fruit, an instant coffee, and my stove, I made my way up to Ford's camp. He looked surprised to see me.

"Well, good morning," he said. He smiled and remained seated inside the door of his tent. He was an older man, I guessed close to retirement age based on his silver hair and scraggly beard, but he looked healthy, if not a little thin. His arms and legs were tan and sinewy, suggesting he was an avid hiker. His eyes were a light hazel color, flashing green one second and golden brown the next.

A couple of chipmunks monitoring Ford's morning meal scattered for cover as I approached. He dug out a spoonful of rehydrated egg from a meal kit and popped it into his mouth. I gave a small smile in return.

"Is this weird? Can I join you for breakfast?" I asked. He nodded.

"No, please, join me. I was hoping we could continue our conversation," he said. I sat on a boulder, using a log round for a table. He looked up, focusing on the side of my head.

"Is your ear alright?" he asked. I had forgotten about my split lobe except when I made the mistake of brushing against it. My hand when up to inspect the torn skin, considering what to say.

"I caught the earring on one of my straps," I lied, heat rising into my cheeks, "tore it right out. Hurt like a son of a bitch. Does it look bad?"

"Well, it doesn't look good. How long ago? We might be able to stitch it," Ford offered. I hesitated.

"I think it's been too long," I replied. "I haven't had time to clean it. There's been a lot to do." Ford nodded.

"The good news is you look like a badass," Ford smiled. I laughed and began setting up my stove to prepare my meal.

"I had a thought," he said, stirring the egg mixture with his long spoon. "I am considering heading up to Sunrise." I liked that he did not hesitate to speak to me like an old friend, casual and inclusive. He explained his final cache was in Sunrise. I ignited my single burner, and it emitted a small *woosh*.

"I am not sure you want to head up there," I replied. "You mentioned Longmire, but it wasn't pretty in Sunrise." I did not meet his eye when I said it. He did not seem to notice.

"So, you came from there?" he asked, interested. I nodded.

"I came back here to stay. I finished my loop in Sunrise, but someone siphoned all the gas out of my car's tank. I tried to drive it but that didn't work out." I hesitated then added, "It didn't feel safe to stay there."

"And you didn't stay at White River?"

"Everything is abandoned. It's eerie and too close to the road."

He nodded. "That was smart." He considered for a moment then continued, "I'm going to run out of food soon. I can try to stretch out what I have. I am hoping there are still caches, mine should be amongst them." I flushed with embarrassment.

"There are a few left. I already raided them, but I am willing to share. There's also the other cache drop in White River, and a lot was abandoned in the campground."

He chuckled as I hurried on to explain.

"I didn't get to do a full check of the store and café. It was too unsettling. The bodies— I planned to go back after I got some rest. It would be nice if someone were there with me."

"Well, that makes two of us. I know we just met, and you don't know me from Adam, but would you like to band together? At least until we find out what is going on?" he asked. "Seems like the world has become a dangerous place."

Right away, I wanted what he offered. It felt right. Something about this man connected to something in me. It was unexplainable.

"I'd like that. How soon do you want to leave?"

With that, we had a plan.

Ford's resilience impressed me. He stopped to admire the wildflowers at the edge of the meadow. He beamed when we set out on the trail. He behaved like it was any day of hiking instead of the aftermath of a pandemic. The ice fields on the mountain shone in the morning sun. A halo of a cloud blew off its peak, rounded like perfectly sculpted icing on top of a boutique cupcake. Mount Rainier was ashen this time of year. Unseasonable heat and a lack of precipitation left the volcano barren, exposing the andesite normally hidden beneath the snow. Ford remarked on its beauty all the same. If his enthusiasm was exaggerated for my benefit, I could not tell. I was happy to have a living person to keep me company.

Su-Jin reappeared as we readied to leave. She had been noticeably missing throughout the morning as Ford and I conversed, sharing the basic information people share when they meet. I had hoped for her continued absence, confirmation her manifestation was only a stress-induced fever dream. She emerged from behind the shelter as we departed, startling me. I could not get used to the sight of her face. Ford remained oblivious. I determined with certainty he did not see her when he turned to look at me, and she stood between us. Ford gave no reaction, and in fact, seemed to look right through her.

Su-Jin managed to keep pace despite her way of sauntering along. I watched her in secret, hoping to see how she caught up. She lagged, walking without a care in the world, and yet we never lost her. Once I picked up my pace, it grew apparent. I could not desert her. She would appear ahead of me on the trail like some kind of strange magic trick. I suspected she was tethered to me, to what extent I did not know, but I could see her attachment to me was outside of her control as much as it was outside of mine. Her annoyed expression every time she was displaced from one spot to another said it all. To make matters worse, her wounds were on full display in the daylight, no shadows to hide what my handiwork had done. She was haunting me. I willed her to disappear and did my best to ignore her presence. Today she was thankfully quiet, and I was grateful.

"How long have you been hiking?" Ford asked, breaking into my thoughts about Su-Jin.

"A little over a year with any seriousness. I adventured a lot as a kid. May as well have grown up outside. But you know how it is when you get older, you get busy, and you don't do the things you love," I replied.

"What made you start again?" he asked. I shrugged.

"It's dumb," I said.

"Try me."

"No, really. It's stupid."

"I promise I won't make fun of you," Ford assured me.

"Do you know the movie *Wild*? I feel like anyone who hikes kind of has to."

He laughed and nodded. "Yes, I do. One of my favorites," he said.

"It was like waking up and realizing I had been asleep for years. My life was stagnant, boring, and all at once, it was killing me. I was part of the machine: work, retire, then die. I felt hopeless, like I wasn't truly living at all. I had nothing to look forward to anymore. I watched it one night. I know it's just a movie, but I couldn't get over that someone really did that. Cheryl decided to do the Pacific Crest then went and hiked it. That resonated with me, the part of me that I was missing. I realized I could do it too. I could hike the PCT. I can do whatever I want. The only person stopping me was me. So why was I?"

"Of course, I was out of shape. I worked at a desk for over a decade. It paid well enough, but it was monotonous: phone calls, emails, and meetings. A lot of hikers I knew used this one spot, a 1000' climb in just over a mile, to prepare for the season. Quite a few conditioned for Wonderland on it. I started going, and it was hard, harder than I thought it would be. But when I reached the peak? It was incredible. I did that, hiked every trail within an hour drive, and started back-packing. I loved putting everything I needed on my back and walking into the woods. Facing the wilderness alone and realizing how capa-ble I had become— I felt strong. I put in for Wonderland on a whim. Thought it would be a good test before I tried one of the big three."

"I think you made the right choice. I've hiked the full loop twenty-seven times, this trip being the twenty-eighth. When I started, permits weren't so hard to get," Ford said. "I run a website dedicated to the trail. We have a few thousand active members. It's a bit of a passion project for me. Frustrating and rewarding at the same time. I hate the administrator role but love the passion for Wonderland. I can't tell you how much I've learned from the people in the group, and I've met several on the trail. You picked a good place to start your long-distance journey. There's nothing quite like Mount Rainier. Those of us who hike here can be a little fanatical about it."

"My goal was to do the Pacific Crest Trail next year," I said. He did a half-turn to look at me, an expression of respect on his face.

"That's impressive, Peri. You said Wonderland was a test. What did you think?" he asked. "Before all this?"

As if to underscore his words, we reached the dead hiker. The contents of his backpack was scattered, the bag torn open by what looked like a small animal or bird. The water bottle remained on its side. Ford paused.

"It's not worth checking out," I told him, continuing to walk by. "I already looked." He regarded me then glanced back at the bushes concealing the body of the young man. Ford fell into step behind me. He was quiet for a time.

"How was your first Wonderland experience?" he asked again, the elation siphoned from his tone.

"I loved it," I said. "I never felt so strong. The trail is hard, but the mountain is breathtaking."

"It's more than that. Tahoma is special," he told me. "All the tribes who lived here considered this to be a sacred place long before Longmire and Vancouver showed up. I would bet you feel it too. Everyone does. This land has immense power. You can't look at that volcano and not feel her presence. The natives thought this was a piece of the spiritual realm here on Earth. I think they are right."

I glanced over at Su-Jin who was admiring a small waterfall along the trail and considered his words. We came upon the huckleberry patch from the day before. Ford stopped to pick the berries. He popped a couple in his mouth, his face puckering.

"Enjoy them while you can," he said, "they won't be here long." I drank water and stretched on the side of the trail, keeping my focus forward and off the huckleberries.

"I had a bunch yesterday, didn't sit well," I replied.

We eventually reached the White River crossing. I hesitated, making a bid to that younger self I had channeled the day before and discovered she was nowhere to be found. The river was high, the bridge vibrating with the force of the current. My breath came out shaky, and I admonished myself. I should be over this hang up by now. Ford noticed.

"Are you alright?" he asked. I looked up from the bridge, caught off guard.

"Yeah, water crossings make me nervous," I replied, embarrassed. "I had a bad experience and it stuck with me."

"Did you fall in?" he asked.

"No, actually. Do you know Echo Lake?" I asked, raising my voice over the river. He nodded.

"It was my first time solo. I prepared for months. I was ready. At Greenwater Lakes, you cross over the river back and forth and the bridges get sketchy the closer you get to the junction for Echo and Lost Lake. There's one that has had repair flags on it for years, but everyone keeps using it. The last bridge before the intersection finally fell into the river. The trail reports warned about it, so I knew. I ran into a couple who were backpacking out of Lost Lake. Before I even asked, they said not to bother fording the river because there was a big log to cross. I figured it would be faster, and I could avoid getting wet. I was so excited to be out there, I didn't think before I did it. I was halfway across when I froze. Looking at the water did something to me. There was no handrail, and the log had this optical illusion like it was too narrow for both of my feet. It felt like I would lose my footing if I continued. I panicked. Then a big group of people came down from the lakes. They were all staring at me. It was awful."

I grew quiet. Ford waited.

"I couldn't make myself move. It was like the fear hijacked my brain. I was absolutely paralyzed. The whole time I can hear one voice telling me to go and the rest is chaos, thoughts rushing as fast as the current below me. A man from that group realized what was happening, and he started to take off his pack to come get me. He was stepping onto the bridge when I finally came to my senses and made it the rest of the way. Afterward, he told me he could see it in my eyes, and he was afraid I would fall when I tried to take the next step. Footbridges were a problem after that. I hoped this trip I would get over it, but it's almost gotten worse. Locking up like that was never part of my makeup, I was never afraid of anything. I grew up next to this river. But I froze and every time I think about it, I panic like I am still standing up there above the river."

"I won't let you fall, hang onto me," Ford said. He went first, placing my hand on his right shoulder and we crossed together. The terror rose in me as we reached the midpoint, my head swam. The water below us made me dizzy. He went slow, and I relaxed when we reached the opposite side. Ford checked in with me before continuing, and I gave a quick thumbs up.

I had shared that story with no one else. It was surprising and a little unexpected how fast I had trusted him. There was a sincerity about Ford, a quality of genuine openness that was hard not to connect with.

We walked up the hill into the campground. It was the same as the day before, empty and abandoned. We passed through in silence.

There was a child's stuffed animal, a light pink fluffy thing covered in dirt and pine needles, discarded on the side of the road. A car in the distance sat with a shattered back window and the passenger door flung open. There were bodies here too. I sensed something harden in myself as I gazed around at the disarray.

"Do you want to check the caches here?" I asked.

"Let's save it, I am not quite ready for this. I understand why you didn't stay here now," Ford said, indicating a child's overturned chair. He did not speak again until we started up the mountain. My calves burned as we ascended through two miles of switchbacks. Ford made it look easy, stepping gracefully into each incline with little exertion. I marveled at the ease with which he moved.

"Why do the Wonderland every year? There are other places and trails, don't you ever get tired of this?" I asked.

"I never get tired of this," he replied, his answer immediate. "I went into business on my own when I was a young man. I did well for myself, but it was a lot of work. While I built the business, I was putting in twelve-hour days, sometimes seven days a week. I missed a lot with my family when the kids were young. I regret that. Eventually, I reached a point where I had solid employees I could trust to manage things so I could start spending more time with my family. I came home to find my wife and children had busy lives of their own. It had taken too long to build it to that point. And they weren't willing to change once I reappeared in their lives," he said the last with a touch of sadness then grew thoughtful.

"I needed something else to fill my time. I started hiking here as a hobby, and it became my church. I grew up with religion but became disenfranchised with it over the years. I always missed having something spiritual to connect with. We live in one of the most beautiful places in the world," he said, his eyes luminous as he spoke. "I will not preach God or religion, but if there is a heaven, I am sure this is it."

I caught a glance of Su-Jin as he spoke. For a moment, she changed. Her caved-in skull vanished, her bulging eye reset. For a flash of a moment, she was her former self. She became whole again. Her hair radiated the shine of the mid-day sun, black and rich, and an aura of color surrounded her. She gave a broad smile, admiration in her eyes.

"Cheonsa," she whispered aloud, giving a shallow bow to this grizzled man who looked as if he might both cry and break out into laughter. Strangely, I understood the word, and I spoke it out loud. *Angel.*

Ford gave me a curious look. "What did you say?" he asked. She had spoken through me. Her word from my mouth.

"Nothing. I misspoke," I replied. With that, Su-Jin shuttered herself and reverted to the broken version of herself. The version I had created.

We reached Sunrise at high noon. It was gloriously hot. I stopped to mop the sweat off my brow and braced myself for what came next. Su-Jin was starting up, her anger coming out. She spoke rapidly into my ear as if she stood at my shoulder. I tried to ignore it, but her words made it hard to focus. She kept mixing English with what I believed was Korean. Not that I knew Korean, but I found myself inexplicably with the knowledge she was speaking the language, and I could understand selected words. None of this made sense to me, which only increased my anxiety. I pressed my lips together, resisting her presence in my mind.

Ford crested the hill ahead of me, stopping when Sunrise came into full view. He was seeing it as I did for the first time. I felt his shock. He looked over the cars left and the bodies decomposing on the baking asphalt. The air thick. I grew nauseous at the sight of Su-Jin's remains. Very little was left. Ford pulled his red handkerchief from his pocket, clasping it over his nose and tying it behind his head. He crossed himself then walked the perimeter of the parking lot in the direction of the Visitor Center. He kept his head down. I did the same, pulling my bandana over my nose and matching his stride. On top of the pit toilet opposite us, a group of crows watched. Their presence ominous, knowing they would feed on me the way they tore apart Su-Jin. One took flight, coming closer to perch on a tree along our path.

"You would think the birds would be—" I trailed off, muffled under the rag.

"For how strong the odor is, I would have expected bears," he replied. "Longmire was much worse." The Sunrise Visitor Center loomed large ahead of us. Its grey shingled roof and two unattached living quarters visible above the trees that surrounded it. It was a beautiful old structure, established when the park service had plans to turn the area into a resort before a railroad deal fell through. The Sunrise Lodge had been built at the same time, planned as a resort, along with two hundred tiny cabins in the surrounding meadows. The cabins were later removed and sold to provide housing for local workers. The Day Lodge was never completed and instead housed the Sunrise Snack Bar and the ranger station.

When Ford braced open the door to the Visitor Center, heat rushed out with the smell of decay in the air. I turned away, the odor worse than before and my stomach gave a hard lurch into my throat. Ford let the door fall shut. He reached into the front pocket of his pack and brought out a tiny jar.

"CBD balm with menthol," he said, swirling a finger around the inside of the jar. "Good for sore muscles and people who don't believe in soap." He rubbed the substance into the cloth covering his face, took another swipe, and rubbed it into mine. The balm made my eyes burn, but it helped. I could no longer smell the rot. We looked absurd, like two thieves on a heist, our presentation in stark relief to the seriousness of our circumstances. We nodded to each other then went inside.

Despite a south facing wall full of windows and it being the middle of the day, it was dim inside. My eyes took a moment to adjust. The dead man remained in the rocking chair before the fireplace or what was left of him. His form had deflated, like it had sunk in on itself, and his skin melted into the wooden seat. His jaw hung slack revealing perfect white teeth and a blackened tongue.

Ford regarded this and crossed himself again. He walked through the fragments of glass to the broken case, touching items as if it were an average day of shopping. He glanced back at me as I hovered near the door. He found the fuel capsules and took two, considered, and included a third.

"We will probably need all of this at some point," he said, referring to the various supplies. "Our stoves will be useless without fuel. There's a storeroom there." He pointed to a backroom across from the case. Beyond the dead man and the fireplace, a hallway led off the main room to another exit. Off the hallway was a stairwell leading to the upper level and another smaller room for storing the rangers hiking gear.

"They used the outer apartments to house volunteers who worked in the park. We should probably check them. I don't know how much they are used anymore. Federal funding for parks has been pretty dismal the last decade or so," Ford said. He scanned the available items as he spoke. I continued to wait by the door.

Every time I looked at the man by the fireplace, I had a crawling sensation up the back of my neck. I imagined he would lurch up from the chair, his skin sagging like an oversized shirt, clinging to his skeleton as he shambled toward me, groaning in the horrible way zombies do. Ford pointed to the door, having found everything he needed, and I made a hasty exit.

Back into the daylight, we looped back to the ranger station where I stored the caches. The crows watched and waited. The room was preserved as I left it, smelling heavily of dust like an antique shop. I pulled the key ring from my pocket and unlocked the closet. Ford walked around the desks as I had the day before, noting the abandoned coffee mug and flipping through the papers left behind. We cleared out what remained in the buckets, and I wonder if any of the people who filled them had survived.

Ford's was present and accounted for, and I found myself relieved I had not taken his cache. That morning, I had only been aware of getting what I needed and getting the hell out of here.

"This is going to be a problem," he said, hands on his slender hips as he cast his gaze over the final pile of food spread out before him. I expected Ford to select a special item from his cache, but instead he lamented the food he had packed.

"What's wrong?" I asked. He looked up at me, a little surprised. He appeared to reconsider before he spoke again then gave up.

"Food," he said, shrugging his shoulders. He loaded the items into his pack. I did not press him further.

Our last stop was the Snack Bar. Upon entering, the humming was all I could hear. If it registered for Ford, he gave no indication. A counter by the door held two carafes for coffee with a third labelled decaf, tiny creamer cups and sugar packets, and an arrangement of pre-packaged pastries, donuts, and cookies. Ford eyed the coffee station and selected a cookie, rattling the plastic cellophane off before stuffing it in his mouth. His eyes rolled back into his head.

This space was the most up to date of the buildings. The café dining area was small, clearly not intended for large groups or heavy traffic. Only six small tables sat in the center of the room with two or four chairs at each. Despite the lodge setting, the furniture and counters were modern.

Below the menu board was a register kiosk and behind that, a kitchen full of stainless-steel countertops and appliances. Braver with a fellow traveler by my side, I slid my pack off next to the register and into the kitchen to explore.

At the back of the room stood a single closed door. I grabbed the handle and, as it swung out, a wall of stench hit me. On the floor of the dry pantry was the body of an older woman whose face was sliding off. Given the mottled condition of her skin and the fluids leaching into her white apron, I suspected she had been here awhile, perhaps longer than the others. She wore a pair of jeans and a t-shirt under her apron with a pinned name tag hanging akimbo. Sandra.

Finding her triggered a reaction in me similar to the one I experienced finding the hiker as I returned to Summerland. Acknowledging the reality of the situation made my heart ache. She had shown up for work, probably not feeling well, and died here instead of at home. It was unfair. She should have been with her family in the end. Instead, she had succumbed to the virus here, alone on the floor. Su-Jin snorted. I half turned and found her standing right behind me.

"You don't care about her," she said, her expression was flat. Her appearance made me wince.

"You like what you see?" she bared her teeth at me. My stomach twisted. I turned back to the pantry, pressing the rag over my mouth the scent overpowering.

Above Sandra's body, the dry storage was filled with food. There were boxes of the pastries stacked on the counter out front, bags of hot dog and hamburger buns, shelf stable condiments, and pre-packaged soups and pastas in need of re-heating. I saw boxes of oyster crackers, salt and pepper packets, bags of snack size chips, and a small assortment of full-sized candy bars.

"Ford!" I called to him, leaving the door open despite Sandra. Next, I opened a large chest freezer, the source of the humming, to find cold condensed air erupting out. Solar power was keeping the cold boxes running. Inside were several boxes of frozen burger patties, bags of French fries and onion rings, and several tubs of ice cream. There were a variety of other bags and boxes buried underneath, but upon seeing the ice cream, I disregarded the rest, sorting through the flavors to locate a tub of rainbow sherbet. When Ford came into the kitchen, I nodded toward the pantry as I plunked the carton on a counter.

"Careful," I said. He winced when he found Sandra, but as his eyes traced upward, he saw the contents inside.

"Now, this we can work with," Ford said, referring to the food. He crossed himself over Sandra and said a prayer under his breath.

After a bit of searching, I found a scoop and a box of waffle cones. I pried the sherbet out of its tub, stuffing each cone full of pink, orange, and green ice. Ford chuckled when he saw me. His eyes crinkled in delight, and I suspected he wore a smile beneath his kerchief.

"You know, it's a rule that ice cream should be enjoyed in the sunshine," Ford said. I agreed.

We carried our cones outside, sitting at a faded and creaking picnic table in a small patch of shade. The sherbet melted fast, so we made quick work of our cones. The sweet flavors coated my mouth, and the heady rush of sugar hit my bloodstream. I relished the treat, knowing it was finite. In this new world, comforts like a hot shower and a cold bowl of ice cream, things I had taken for granted my entire life, would soon become unattainable luxuries.

Ford licked a drip on the side of his cone, took a big bite, and sighed happily. Our sentiments were the same. The crows regarded us with deep interest. Ford broke off bits of the golden cone to toss to them.

"Don't feed the animals," I said halfhearted through a mouthful of blissfully cold lime sherbet. Ford shrugged. "They have relied on our garbage a long time. They will have to go back to their instincts."

He considered then added, "When our supplies run out, so will we."

There was enough in the café to buy us time. Along with the pantry and the freezer, there were a few cold boxes storing fresh produce such as apples, oranges, a few kiwis, a tub of cut up pineapple, and a variety of lettuce and salad vegetables. There were several packages of sliced cheese, some questionable lunchmeat, as well as milk and eggs. When the café had been remodeled, someone must have had the foresight to connect its power into to the solar battery as a backup. I wondered how long it would last.

"How many more miles do you have in you today?" Ford asked. His tone suggested he had an idea.

"Well, it is ten miles back to Summerland," I replied, popping the last bit of my cone into my mouth.

"How about an adventure?"

Hours later, I sat on the scaffold of the Mount Fremont fire lookout while a very fat chipmunk harassed me. I offered him a carrot stick from my lunch. The rodent accepted the carrot, sniffed, then discarded it. Ford held out a raw almond, which the chipmunk took without hesitation and scurried off.

"Don't feed the animals," I said to Ford. He smiled and alternately kicked his feet over the ledge of the platform like a child on a swing. Beyond, we overlooked Grand Park where a herd of mountain goats, tiny white dots from this vantage, languished in the fading summer sun. Rolling hills of forest extended as far as the eye could see, but the true glory was Mount Rainier. It had to be the most famous view in the entire park. Ford proclaimed it was his favorite place.

"I know its touristy," he said, a bit sheepish while we were walking the last half mile to the lookout, the scree sounding like broken plates beneath our feet.

The chipmunk, or perhaps another that looked like the first, and just as fat, returned. He grappled and tested the various clasps and zippers on my pack. I shooed him away. Ford flipped another almond in the animal's direction. I shot him a look, and he shrugged in response.

"This is a no judging zone, Peri. We can all pretend we don't feed the squirrels, but let's face it: everyone feeds the squirrels or they would be skinny squirrels," he said, indicating to another chipmunk lurking on his side of the deck. He passed that chipmunk an almond too, and we watched as it buried the nut into its cheek pouch. I tossed the abandoned carrot down to the rocks below where I had seen ground squirrels and chipmunks less brazen than the ones surrounding us.

Su-Jin milled around beneath us, refusing to climb the stairs to the platform. I sensed she was afraid of heights and felt a small pang of guilt, unsure why she had not used the opportunity to disappear like she had so many times before. I dismissed her feelings, remembering how she had sneered at me in the café.

As we sat at a picnic table spoiling our dinners, Ford had suggested we stay the night at the lookout rather than make the trek back to Summerland.

"Imagine! The once in a lifetime chance to spend the night in a fire lookout in Mount Rainier National Park!" he exclaimed. Standing up from the table, he spread his arms wide like a circus ringmaster showcasing the final act. As if to add to that point, he went on, "Behold! Witness the greatest sunset of all time!"

I was, of course, sold.

He followed his grandstanding with what would become a favored punchline of ours, an attempt to find the bright side of surviving the apocalypse.

"What else do you do when you are the last two people on Earth?" he asked and then answered, "Whatever you want."

My excitement felt like wearing a jacket two sizes too small, ill-fitting, and strange, but it was something to keep me warm. It felt inappropriate to experience a bit of happiness at the end of the world. I did not fight the opportunity and instead packed a few pieces of fruit and a collection of vegetables from the produce I found in the café. It was impractical, but after eating freeze-dried meals and granola bars for almost two weeks, I craved fresh food.

Ford dozed as I basked like a lizard on the deck enjoying the warmth of the sun on my skin. The day passed, and the air cooled. We both roused when the evening breeze picked up. I pulled out my sleeping bag and wrapped it around my sunscreen sticky arms, watching the sun begin its descent below the horizon. A calm settled over us as the golden hour arrived, and a palette of colors in every shade of red and orange were thrown against the canvas of a deepening blue sky. Stars lit, one by one, faint at first and then shimmering in brilliance from galaxies far, far away.

While the sunset was expected, the show after dark was not. The air grew colder, and we remained. Throughout the day, we had noticed a hazy grey-brown cloud rising in the distance. After the sun dipped below the horizon, we realized the plume was smoke. A bright orange light spanned the skyline from what we guessed was Tacoma, and the city was burning. It confirmed that what was happening to the world outside of the park was unknown. Now the only light in the sky was cast by the stars overhead. I had not witnessed a deeper night. With the glare from the cities gone, the sky was a riot of distant suns. The Milky Way, a current of sparkling diamonds, laced through a glowing river of white cold radiance.

"To think, this is what the first people used to see when they looked up at the sky," Ford said. I could not see his face in the darkness but felt the warmth of his presence and the power of his awe. "Looking at this, it is hard for me to believe there is no such thing as design."

"I think how many of those are stars with their own systems with planets like ours. How many other people, or life that may not even resemble humanity, are looking out at the sky asking the same questions? It makes me feel small. Humans think they are unique, but I find it unbelievable that we would be alone when the universe is infinite," I replied. "If we are so special, how can it end like this? The universe is a cold place where things happen without meaning. People strive to be memorialized, to do something important, but it won't matter when we are all gone. This planet will wipe the slate clean like we never existed. I think we want to believe in God simply because we assume we are special, that our species is treasured, and our existence is not meaningless. I think it is everyone's hope to become a part of time. To be remembered."

"You may be right," Ford said. At that moment, a flash of green and yellow arched across the blackness. A shooting star.

"Oh! Did you see that?" I asked. When I looked at Ford, I could almost see the pinpoints of light reflected in his eyes.

"You are lucky I did. It doesn't count unless two people see it," he said. "Of course, in my time, when we would stay up to watch the meteorite showers it had to be a rule because there was usually some kind of substance involved. When that was the case, we saw a lot of interesting things." We both laughed.

"Thank you for coming here with me, Peri," Ford said. "I know we just met, and we aren't in the best of circumstances. I am not trying to be insensitive, but being here tonight feels like a blessing to me."

"Ford, what do you think about staying here?" I interjected. Another meteorite skimmed across the sky, its brightness lit our faces.

"You mean the tower?"

"No," I said. "What do you think about staying in the park? My plan, at first, was to get home, but I wonder what would even be there for me. I guess I don't know how it will be much different than stay-ing here."

"I wonder about my children. My ex-wife. I don't know how I would reach them. What about your family? Parents? Children?" he asked.

"No husband or kids. My parents separated after my brother died which was ages ago. My dad passed a couple years back. My mom and I don't spend much time together. She was never the same after my brother—" I trailed off. "Her and I were never close."

"I'm sorry," Ford said.

"Oh, that's just how it was. Like I said, it was a long time ago. I don't have anyone to get back to," I replied. It hurt to say it out loud. I was alone. I had been alone before the end of the world. For a moment, I sat with the emotion, a familiar pain, one I had grown comfortable with over the years. I buried it in my consciousness like a box of old photographs forgotten in the attic.

"I think it's safe to say we aren't sick. I am assuming we were both exposed. At least, I know I was which leads me to believe you can have a natural immunity or be asymptomatic," I said, not bothering to clarify my exposure came from my encounter with Su-Jin. If she were a carrier, I would be sick or dead by now. As for Su-Jin, it was clear she had been surrounded by people who were infected, and I could not recall her showing any outward symptoms of illness. Animals had consumed Su-Jin's body, but the corpses of the afflicted had remained untouched.

"Come to think of it, I was exposed before I started the trail. In Mowich, there was a woman there who was clearly ill. She came off Wonderland with assistance from her group. They had started in Sunrise, so maybe their second or third day? Her group was adamant her water filter failed. I remember thinking it was odd how fast it hap-pened. Only a matter of days. Giardia can take weeks before you have symptoms, but they asked a ranger to call an ambulance for her. I helped load her into the ambulance. I assume it is airborne based on how fast it moves. I did not come into direct contact with anyone in Longmire, but I had to get my cache there. It was worse than Sunrise or White River." Ford did not say anything else after that. What he had seen had affected him so much he avoided the subject. He was not willing to share the story, and I was not going to press him.

"I know you know this, but there are more cache locations. White River, Mowich," I said, redirecting the conversation. "There are all the campgrounds and so much still to explore in Sunrise. And Paradise. We have everything we need to stay out here and at least get our bearings. If there are two people who are prepared to face this, it is definitely us. We will have to find clothes for winter. Food is going to be a concern at some point, but even with those things in mind, I am firm we would faire far better here than trying to go back to the city."

Ford considered this then said, "If we survived in here, people survived out there."

"Exactly," I said. I did not need to continue the natural line of that conversation. It had been unspoken between us from the moment he arrived in Summerland and saw me holding the hatchet. I knew I was lucky it was Ford who showed up. A different person might have stolen what I had or worse. Desperate people do desperate things. And there were still people out there. The fact that Ford and I were alive was evidence enough. I knew Su-Jin factored in too. There would be others.

"Is there are any chance your family is out there waiting for you?" I asked.

He was quiet for a long time, so long I thought he had fallen asleep. When he spoke next, I realized he was holding back tears.

"No," he replied. "No. I don't think anyone is waiting for me." He sniffled a little, I wanted to reach out and take his hand but felt he would pull away if I did. This was a deeper pain for him, and it made us the same. I never quite belonged, feeling separate from the people around me. I long held out hope there would be someone who understood me and what existed in my heart, but over time, that wish faded each time that friendship and love was not reflected in another person. Loneliness is the death of connection.

"There is no other place on Earth I would rather be than here.

I live for this park. This mountain is my one true love. Wonderland is my home. I would happily spend another season here with you," Ford said.

I smiled at this. Perhaps it was strange. Two people with a thirty-year age difference, perfect strangers, choosing to shelter together, but these were strange days. Perhaps borne out of fear or a lack of other options, I hoped our chance meeting would grow into friendship. I felt like, maybe, it already had.

"Let's stay, Peri."

Feeling for it in the dark, he took my hand. I squeezed it in return. A connection. We stayed long into the night watching the stars fall against the backdrop of a galaxy lit Tahoma, like a ghost ship on a distant horizon.

August gave way to September, and we made our home in Mount Rainier National Park. It was less of a hardship than expected to be cut off from what was left of society. I could spend my time as I chose which was a complete turnaround from my former life living the nine to five grind. I did not miss hearing jokes about Mondays, or meetings that could have been an email, or coming home exhausted despite sitting at a desk all day. I woke when I wanted, and I was beholden only to myself. There was no supervisor to explain myself to. For the first time since I was a kid, I felt like I had a measure of freedom. Other days, I wished for the amenities of modern culture I no longer had, like a hot shower. At least once a day, I missed the ability to take a shower. We scavenged supplies and hiked mountains. Humanity's worst nightmare became my dream come true.

Ford and I made camp at the Sunrise Campground along the Wonderland Trail. It was tucked a mile away from the Visitor Center into the backside of Yakima Park. I was still wary of being close to the road, but Sunrise was the best location to begin the project of gathering and inventorying supplies so we could remain in Mount Rainier.

The first matter to attend to was body removal. We started with

Sandra. I sourced heavy dishwashing gloves and vinyl aprons from the kitchen. The Visitor Center had a supply of N95 masks and old jumpsuits from an old custodial crew. We donned the jumpsuits then added on the gloves, aprons, and masks. Using a tarp we found in storage, we carefully rolled Sandra's body onto it and carried her outside into the balmy heat. Ford was adamant about burying her. I had mixed feelings.

"They have been trying to restore this meadow for the better part of the last century, Ford. I don't think we should dig a hole here. The animals aren't touching the bodies," I said.

"She deserves a proper burial," he said.

"Okay, humor me this? What if she didn't want to be buried? How do you know?" I asked.

"The cross around her neck tells me she would want to be buried," he replied. I conceded to his point. Ford produced shovels from out of the depths of the Visitor Center, and we dug her a grave. Excavating the hole took an entire day, the hardpan fighting us for every inch. Our shovels found stones and boulders requiring we pry them loose to continue. We persisted and eventually dug a shallow grave. As we laid Sandra in, the heel of her shoe caught the edge of the hole and the skin nearly slid off her foot along with the sneaker. Ford was horrified. After that, he did not insist on burying the others.

The man in the rocking chair had dribbled small puddles of fluid onto the floor in front of the hearth. We carried him out, chair and all. Full decomposition was at work. His body was loose, his arms dangled, and his flesh sagged. The way his head rolled from side to side as we heaved his body out of the building made me worry it might snap off. We carried him to the far end of the lot, like a sentinel guarding the entry, positioning him to face the mountain. Ford said a short prayer to which I stood by solemn. Su-Jin observed throughout. She whispered "amen" after Ford did and crossed herself along with him. I had no such religious sentiments.

We bleached the floor where the puddles accumulated, then I rolled a display about meadow restoration over the top of it to cover the staining on the floor. We never moved that display. Even when, later, we pushed back all of the others to sleep close to the fireplace, that one remained.

After the spaces were sufficiently cleared out, we began our scavenging project in earnest. It was lucky for us to find a half-full box of gas cannisters in the storeroom as we relied on our camp stoves on the trail. The old volunteer quarters were sparse, looking like college dorms, each with a striped mattress, a single dresser, and a mirror. They stored historical display items: dusty framed photographs, cases of plant life and volcanic matter, and piles of out-of-date literature.

We found clothing for both of us. Some of it dated, but for our purposes, it would work. The fashion police were noticeably absent for the apocalypse, and neither of us cared much about appearances. Ford wore the same shirt for five days at one point. The clothes just had to function. Knowing rain would come, and snow would follow, we hunted for heavy jackets and found them in the backroom where all the trail gear was kept. We sorted through every pack used for ranger hikes, selecting the best supplies from what we found and what we ourselves carried. We inventoried the rest and stored it in case we needed it later.

We checked the vehicles left in the lot, donning our makeshift hazmat suits. The bodies we found were too decomposed to disturb, so they remained as we found them. Ford said a small prayer for each. It was strange finding money, wallets, purses, and cell phones; things once of value, now rendered useless in this new reality.

I took a cord from one of the cars to charge my phone in the kitchen of the Snack Bar. The solar battery ran the fridge and freezer, and I was able to use the outlets to give my phone a charge. I do not know what I hoped for. A signal? A message from someone from my old life? The phone gave nothing except a further sense of how alone we were. I kept it, although it was impractical, and used it to take at least one picture every day, marking the moments I wanted to capture. Perhaps it was sentiment, a tether to my former life. Ford made jokes about my generation's obsession with technology. I called him grandpa.

We found more food in the vehicles, mostly snacks. It was like a treasure hunt; we never knew what kind of treats we might find. One car had a whole tote full of snacks along with a first aid kit, a knee brace, and other random items. I respected the person's readiness and love of the trail that they built an entire box to ensure they could leave for a hike at a moment's notice. The snack tote had a bag half-full of stale marshmallows. I insisted on a small campfire at the campground so we could roast them.

"It's too dry to be doing this," he said, monitoring the fire. Temperatures were still reaching eighty degrees during the day as we arrived at September's midpoint. There had only been a few separate occasions of rain in weeks. I pointed to the bucket of water beside me.

"We are being careful and besides that, it's cold here at night," I said. He wanted to object, so I pulled out my ace in the hole.

"What do you do when you are the last people on Earth?" I asked him. He frowned at me then said nothing.

"Whatever we want," I finished. Any anxiety Ford had about the fire did not stop him from enjoying his share of burnt marshmallows. Having plundered Sunrise for its goods, we agreed it was time to search another location.

Where Sunrise was open and airy, the White River Campground was restless and unsettled. The wind added to the effect, blowing hot air through the tree branches, and rustling abandoned tents. The campground was situated in a canyon that funneled a near constant current of air. It was hard to get used to, the sound of the wind unnerved me. Despite this, we made the temporary move as we scavenged the area for supplies.

There were not as many of the dead as I expected to find. White River had largely been abandoned. Despite September moving rapidly into October, during the day temperatures remained in the high seventies to low eighties without a drop of precipitation. Nature was taking its course, the ongoing heat accelerating decomposition, and the bodies no longer resembled anything close to a living, breathing person.

We accumulated an impressive store of food. What was left behind in the two RVs could have fed the whole campground for a few nights. The first RV was empty of any remains, seeming abandoned by whoever it had belonged to, and had a full propane tank, so we moved in. The days were hot, but the nights were getting colder. We ate like kings for a short time. Ford packed down elk burgers to pan fry on the range. The house on wheels came equipped with an oven, which I used to bake fries and onion rings pilfered from the freezer in the Snack Bar. We ate the burgers like a steak, covered in seasoning with a side of fries and sliced apples. I savored each bite. The fries were the perfect touch.

The other trailer was occupied, but the residents were no longer with the living. Su-Jin stood outside as I approached it on our third day at White River, shaking her head, and waving me away.

"Not this one," she kept saying. "Not this one. Darkness here."

Despite her objections, which I could not exactly present to Ford, we investigated. She waited on the steps of the trailer, peering inside in a way that made me uncomfortable. Her warnings were founded.

We discovered a family of three in the master bedroom at the back. Two adults on the bed with the child between them. They held each other, reminding me of the casts of Mount Vesuvius' victims in Pompeii. From the bodies alone the cause of death was impossible to tell. They were in advanced decomposition and beginning to liquify, the bed absorbing the fluid. If they had been sick, there was no way to know. Su-Jin provided an answer.

"They not sick," she called, as I stood over the bodies. "They choose."

I found the bottle of extended-release oxycodone and the powder of crushed pills on the kitchen counter, confirming Su-Jin's words. They had antibiotics too, and I took both bottles. Ford found a sheet to spread over the family. He said a long prayer, lingering there with his head hung in silence, then shut the door, cutting off the bedroom from the main area.

We went through the trailer once and never returned. Along with an assortment of pantry items like pastas and jarred sauces and children's snacks, we found an unopened box of saltines. The label alone triggered a memory of teaching my little brother, Bryce, how to spread peanut butter on the crackers when he was only four. Our mother abhorred sugary snacks, but we had access to honey and the white sugar our father used for his coffee, so we drizzled honey over our saltines and added spoonfuls of sugar to our cereal. One afternoon, I had forgotten to wash his hands, and he had patted our fat tabby with sticky palms. He had laughed with delight, holding his hand up to me, wiggling his fingers, and squealing "Fur fingers, Beri!" Unable to pronounce the 'p' as a toddler, his name for me stuck. The recollection was bittersweet. Later, when I opened the saltines, I thought of the dead child in the trailer, and I thought of my brother.

We found an assortment of useful gear like a tabletop camp stove and the small green bottles of propane. There was an extensive wardrobe in the second RV including thermals and heavy jackets for winter. The men's clothing was too large for Ford, but it would work. The women's clothing fit me near perfect.

The pièce de résistance was a collapsible wagon we found in the trunk of a car. It was the kind of wagon people used for a lake day or to tote their children around a theme park with cloth sides and sturdy wheels. The amount of excitement Ford exhibited over the wagon seemed inordinate.

"Oh my god, what is the big deal?" I said. "We have backpacks. It's going to be a pain in the ass to take that thing on the trail. It will be too wide for certain sections, but especially pulling it uphill. Leave it."

"No, Peri, you'll see. This thing will be worth its weight in gold," he said, pulling it out to admire it.

He reminded me by repeating the statement every time we used it. Later, I would begrudgingly admit he was right that the damned thing was worth its weight in gold. We stacked loads of food and supplies inside, strapped it all down with a ratty blanket and a couple bungee cords, and trucked it up the mountain. Moving it uphill was a two-man operation, but it reduced the number of trips to transport the gathered provisions.

In an old hippie van with a putrefied corpse in the back, Ford discovered a handgun.

"There's always a rule breaker," he said, checking the weapon to verify if it was loaded and found it was. He flipped the safety. I stood back, eyeing the gun.

"Are you comfortable with me hanging on to this?" he asked. I considered.

"I don't like guns," I replied.

"Do you know how to shoot one?" he asked.

"In theory," I said.

"If we find more bullets, you need to know how." He tucked the gun away.

"Over my dead body," I replied, walking away. He did not ask for an explanation, and I did not offer one. We never found any more bullets.

Before we left White River for good, we took an impromptu side trip to Indian Bar. After passing through Summerland, we climbed to the top of Panhandle Gap. The way through straddles a ridgeline across loose rocks and pumice. Snow frequently covers it even during the warmer months.

The quality of the snowpack was worse than when I had come through weeks prior. The midday heat had warmed the snow to slush that provided no traction. Boot indentations from dozens of hikers marked the passage of time. The footprints encased in the ice layer gathering pools of melt water under the glare of the sun. We carefully picked our way along the trail, the ground below falling away. There would be no recovering from a stumble here.

"How the hell did you do this in the dark? This would be nothing but ice," I asked, taking a cautious step. Ford tossed an impish grin over his shoulder.

"Very carefully," he replied. "I wasn't thinking to be honest. I'd already come too far when I realized what I had gotten myself into. I was single-minded that night. It's one of those things you don't really think about until after you've done it and realize it was stupid. I have plenty of stories like that."

"I hiked Dirty Harry's Balcony early last season. There was still a lot of snow at higher elevations, so I asked people coming out if I should bring my microspikes. This guy told me I didn't need them, and like an idiot I took his word for it. It was hands down the worst hike I have ever done. The trail was a literal sheet of ice near the top and trying to descend— forget it. What a nightmare. If I had worn my spikes, it would have been a piece of cake. One spot, I thought I could slide down on my butt. That was a mistake! I went sideways, ended up tangling with a tree, and wound up with road rash all over my hands," I replied.

We continued to tell tales of our misadventures in the backcountry as we navigated the treacherous section. It felt precarious being that high up with the ground sinking below our steps without warning. Ford fell near the end of our descent where the quality of the snow was no better than ice cream and received a gash on his knee.

The view from this vantage was otherworldly, stretching for hundreds of miles in all directions, and along with Rainier, we could see St. Helens and Mount Adams to the south. Eventually, we descended between scattered clusters of trees, the mountain disappearing below the crest of the Cowlitz Divide. Threads of snow clung to the crags between the grey washed stone of the razorback peaks, the rock face of the ridge eroded over time from the barrage of wind and water.

Before us was a valley of emerald-green meadows tucked below the Divide's serrated edge. It was like nowhere else in the park. A wash of stone poured down the center, surrounding the grey blue of the Ohanapacosh River. Next to the river sat the old stone group shelter which had long withstood the test of time and weather.

After the strain of the climb and the oppressive heat, I felt a swell of happiness to return to this place of such captivating beauty. Indian Bar felt more akin to an alpine meadow in Switzerland than anywhere in America.

Following our arrival, we languished next to a cold rushing creek in the shadow of a copse of trees the rest of the day. Late-season wildflowers raised their colored heads to the sun. It felt like heaven. Most itineraries for Wonderland are nine to ten days, which means never getting to stay too long in one spot when you are a circuit hiker. Coming back was worth the effort it took to truly experience the remote and picturesque location.

As we relaxed, whiling away the afternoon, the sun drifted across the open sky. Ford turned to me.

"Do you have a trail name?" he asked. I was leaning back against a boulder with one foot in the creek, my eyes closed.

"No," I replied, peering out from under one of my lids.

"You are going to need one," he said, thoughtful.

"Aren't these things supposed to come naturally?" I asked. "Like you set up camp next to a deer carcass and a cougar tries to eat you, so you 'earn' the nickname 'Cougar Bait'?"

Ford acted like he was considering, a mischievous grin on his face then held up a finger like an idea had struck him.

"Hatchet!" he said.

"Hatchet?" I asked.

"Our first meeting. Peri's weapon of choice," Ford laughed. I pursed my lips acting frustrated but could not hold back my amusement. When I did not object, Ford nodded.

"That's the one. Hatchet." he smiled.

We returned to White River after staying several days in Indian Bar but only to move the last of the supplies we found to the Sunrise Visitor Center. Despite what horrors happened there, our high fortress was as close to a home as we had now. I was ready to get back. Even though the days were warm, the nights were too cold to sleep outside comfortably. More than once in Indian Bar, one or both of us had woken shivering. Ford succeeded in sourcing firewood and built a small fire in the stone hearth each evening to help heat the large room. He did it was some anxiety, the dry weather presented potential dangers. We kept our fires low and prayed for rain.

In between scavenging and compiling resources, I continued to hike. Once we had agreed to stay, I took full advantage of having unfettered access to the park. Sometimes Ford joined me, and other times, I went alone. The Burroughs was a favorite place of mine. The Burroughs formation was built from remnants of an old lava flow during one of Rainier's more active periods. It was undersold as a hike. Everyone suggested the more popular Fremont Lookout. I remembered being told how hard it was, many finding the exposure on the barren landscape a deterrent for casual hikers. I suspected an effort was made to keep this trail a secret from tourists. The mountain was its most glorious from the Third Burrough. It felt like you could reach out and touch the volcano. The trail became so familiar to me, I memorized each ridge and glacier on Rainier's north face. It was the face of the mountain I had grown to know from my childhood home. We often ventured back to the Fremont lookout to catch the sunsets.

As the days stacked without rain, a brown haze settled over the surrounding hills, casting them in faded colors. The fire in Tacoma still burned. Ford considered a move to the lookout as the days wore on and the smoke grew thicker. With air conditions worsening and the ongoing drought, we stopped building fires despite the cold at night. Ford feared a single spark would ignite the tinderbox surrounding us.

No one in the Pacific Northwest ever acclimated to fire season, although it was a problem we dealt with for decades. It felt anomalous that the wettest part of the country would burn at the end of every summer. The world would watch as the fires raged on. These were not the summers of my youth.

When I was an adolescent, regular precipitation would continue through the Fourth of July. A dry Fourth was rare, the rain was so common it was part of the tradition. After the holiday, the sun would finally appear, and for those few remaining weeks, summer days would reign. People would crowd the lakes to beat the heat or linger in parks to enjoy the sun. It was time to pull out the shorts, tank tops, and summer dresses from the back of the closet, the smell of sunblock heavy in the air. It was the season for barbeques, late-night bonfires, and swimming pools.

In stark opposition, the summers of my adulthood were fire bans, red flag warnings, and toxic smoke. I do not know when things changed, only that they did. It was indisputable despite the fervent objections of the climate change deniers. Our world had moved on. It was different from the one I had grown up in. Summers brought masks, burning eyes, closed roads, and evacuations. We had gone too far if this was the outcome. On some level, if what Ford said was true, I understood why the terrorists had loosed this virus upon us. We took our world for granted. The endless summer on Mount Rainier would confirm it when the fires moved in.

Storms came and what they lacked in rain, they made up for with electricity. We endured high, hot winds and voltage filled clouds. Lightning fractured against the sky and thunder followed. Rain would begin to fall, enough to dampen the surface of the soil and no more. The parched earth sucked it up in minutes. We watched the turbulent weather from the safety of the Visitor Center.

On a night in mid-October, a tempest came through unlike any I had seen before. The air around us was a continuous reverberation punctuated by the occasional earth-shaking thunderclap. The system spanned miles, and Sunrise felt like the epicenter. Lightning flashed around us in all directions, seconds apart, bolts tore through the swollen purple clouds like whip cracks. From time to time, a discharge would illuminate the sky on its path to earth, tearing through the darkness and threatening to rip the night open. I watched from a window, the hair on my arms stood visibly on end. The air itself was electric. I showed Ford, and he cautioned me away from the glass. I tried to sleep but found myself restless, awoken each time a cannon blast rocked the building.

I woke the following morning to a dense haze, thicker than what we had grown used to. The smell of woodsmoke permeated the air. A fire was close.

"It's bad today," I told Ford who was already awake and eating breakfast in the cafe. He looked at me over a packaged cinnamon bun and the last of the huckleberries. The sight of them made me nauseous. For my own breakfast, I selected a can of peaches and popped the top, slurping the sugary syrup. I turned my back to him, looking out the window instead.

"I am heading out to Fremont," he said. "I need to see where this is coming from."

"I'm coming with," I said. After finishing our meal, we hiked out to the lookout with only our water bottles and a single pair of binoculars. The bandanas covered our faces to help filter the air. The mountain was cloaked in a brown fog, and the distant hills were almost invisible except as faint outlines. After last night's fireworks, I knew what we would find.

Fremont was built on a point overlooking a vast stretch of forest land. It had long served as a working fire lookout although infrequently used. It was the best vantage we had to locate the source of the smoke. The weather had been too warm for too long, and without the benefit of a good rain shower in weeks, the groundcover and trees were fuel waiting to be ignited.

As it would turn out, we had good reason to worry. The last quarter mile revealed a dark cloud of smoke rising beyond the tower. As we approached, we could see it was close, originating from the ridge opposite ours.

"Is that Huckleberry Creek?" I asked. Ford scanned the surrounding mountains using the binoculars.

"Close, it looks like Lake Eleanor. It doesn't look like it's made it over the peaks, but it's coming," Ford replied.

"And when it does?" I asked as he handed me the binoculars. I scanned for the fire line and found nothing. It was a sizeable blaze based on the expanse of smoke. I lowered the binoculars.

The burn would progress unchecked. We could hope it was being pushed into the valley away from us, but the wind was telling a different story which was why we were surrounded by smoke. When it crested the ridge, the fire would have to travel across the Cold Basin before it arrived at our doorstep. That bought us time but how much was only a guess.

"We should go," Ford said. He searched my face for agreement. We could not risk being trapped here. The thought of trying to escape with a forest fire at our backs was frightening. I nodded. We were resolute it was time to leave the place we had made our home.

Sunrise was never the final solution. We knew when winter came, and it would come, this place would be buried under fifty feet of snow. We had lingered too long here, expecting the first snowfall to drive us out.

Longmire was set to be our winter retreat. It sat at the lowest elevation in the park, only 2700' above sea level, and maintained better amenities than were available in Sunrise. There would be more resources there, and if we planned to last the winter, we would need everything we could find. The location presented a new problem: the possibility of people. That was assuming Longmire was not already occupied. It was a risk we would have to take. There was no other choice except to move or leave the park. We would not survive in Sunrise.

Returning to the Visitor Center, we gathered what we would need to head into the backcountry. Before a trip, backpackers spend countless hours calculating their base weight to ensure their load will be manageable to carry over the required distance. We crammed that consideration down to mere minutes, spreading everything out on the center's floor to look over it quickly. Food was the priority. We were determined to bring as much as we could, but there was no way to take it all. Choices had to be made.

Su-Jin stood by the fireplace, silently watching as we considered each item in turn. We agreed to share a tent to carry more fuel. We discarded the bulk of our summer clothes. There was a spirited discussion over discarding our sleeping pads, but we thought better of it. Carrying additional weight would be uncomfortable after sleeping on the cold, hard ground.

I filtered out the luxuries I had carried on Wonderland: a thin paperback novel, the remnants of my personal hygiene supplies, and last, my cell phone. I wanted to keep it, the photographs meant something to me; both the ones from before the virus and the ones I had taken to record our time here. Ford regarded my hesitation while he re-loaded his pack.

"If we can't use it, don't bring it," he said. I frowned, placing it in my pocket, unsure.

There was a decision to be made regarding our trajectory. The shorter distance was to travel clockwise through Summerland and Indian Bar to reach Longmire but would necessitate another crossing over Panhandle Gap which had already proven to be treacherous the last time we had navigated the area.

"It's nearly double the miles to take the westside route," Ford said, rubbing the back of his neck.

"Do you think we can make it with the wagon over the pass with the snow still up there?" I asked. The thought of attempting Panhandle with our planned haul was unnerving, but the additional mileage was a considerable disadvantage as well. Neither felt like a good option at that moment.

"I don't think we should chance it. I'm not sure we can get the wagon through. It's sketchy, and I'm not willing to risk losing the food or falling to get there faster," Ford said after deep consideration. "If we got stuck and had to turn around, we would be heading straight into the fire. We'd end up travelling the same miles and more. I'm not willing to gamble on that. The west side has plenty of camps and patrol cabins, we can break up the journey into smaller pieces. If the weather turns, and it likely will, we'll be grateful for those cabins. We won't have to wake up in a puddle every day."

We packed the wagon and filled the extra spaces in our backpacks with food. What we had in Sunrise was sufficient for a few months, but there was no way to carry all of it. Using the wagon would slow us down considerably, at times requiring we both carry it through difficult and rough terrain, but it was the only way to pack more than a few days' supply. Our packs would be heavy, and not all the food we had sourced was designed to be lightweight for backpacking. We had a challenging trip ahead of us.

The smoke grew worse. The sky took on a faint orange hue that felt alien, the atmosphere like a day on Mars rather than here on Earth.

Ash began to fall from the sky as we made our final preparations, a thin layer dusting the cars and sidewalk. Flakes fell into Su-Jin's black hair like snow. It was our signal to go. The air was hard to breathe. We replaced the bandanas with the N-95 masks we had found, keeping the kerchiefs damp to wipe the soot from our eyes.

"We can make it to Granite Creek before dark, but I don't think that will get us out of the smoke," Ford said, standing over the three-dimensional map of the park. The wagon was loaded, our packs filled as full as we could get them. I worried I would not be strong enough to carry it the distance we needed to go but said nothing.

"Then we press for Mystic and hope the canyon gives us wind," I said. We agreed on the course, knowing we would be hiking after darkness fell. I had one final task. I returned to the café and went into the kitchen. We had stored the remainder of our food supplies here, hoping placing it in the steel cabinetry and appliances would protect it if the fire reached the Day Lodge. I placed my phone inside the fridge with the charging cord. I stopped at the door exiting the café, considering.

"It time to go," Su-Jin urged me on. "Now." There was no anger in her request, only urgency, and I felt no frustration toward her. She was afraid and so was I.

"Okay," I said, leaving the last artifact of my former life behind.

We tried to move fast while dragging the wagon, the food inside strapped down. We left behind more than either of us felt comfortable with, not knowing what we would find on the other end of our journey. I quickly became covered in soot. The sweat cleared tracks of it down the side of Ford's face. Su-Jin remained spotless aside from the ash in her hair, her strange magic at work.

It was like walking through a nightmare, the sky blood red as the fire grew. We were surrounded by toxic, unbreathable air as the ash of burnt trees fell from the sky. Smoke overwhelmed the trail. Visibility was poor.

We reached the spur trail for Skyscraper Mountain and took the quarter mile detour to gauge the fire's distance a final time. It was an unpleasant climb. Smoke burnt my eyes. Upon reaching the top, visible flames were moving along the ridgeline at the peak of Scarface Mountain. The same southerly wind that overwhelmed us with smoke was propelling the wildfire down into Grand Park. The distance between us and the expanding inferno was nearly eight miles, but I feared if the flames jumped the Cold Basin or the western fork of the White River, Wonderland would burn. There might not be much left in Sunrise to return to if the blaze made it that far.

We set the fire at our backs and put the miles behind us. Upon reaching Granite Creek, I splashed cold water on my face, neglecting to filter and not caring. Ford did the same. My eyes stung from the carcinogenic air. My nose, despite the protection, was congested, and my breath was short. We kept moving.

The moon came up, crimson and swollen. It was like passing through the hellscapes of Mordor: Rainier, a real-life Mount Doom, glowed a fiery red as the vermillion sun set. When darkness fell, the sky glowed the burgundy of wine, lit from below by the expanding fire. We did not speak, finding it hard to breathe through the masks as we marched and impossible to get oxygen without them. From the distance of Winthrop Creek, we saw the fire moving into Grand Park. Tomorrow a black scar would be left in its place. My eyes watered. I was unsure if it was from the burning smoke or my devastation that the wildfire would destroy this beautiful place.

We relied on our head lamps through the darkness. The air improved as we moved out of the smoke's path. It was a relief to be in good air again. The smoke was suffocating and claustrophobic. Exhaustion plagued me those final miles. Pulling the wagon with so little usable oxygen had taken its toll. Ford's energy was flagging as well. He tripped over roots and kicked rocks, fighting to keep from dragging his feet. He cursed with every stumble. We pushed through despite the struggle. We tried to encourage each other and failed, both of us reaching our limits. We fell mute, no words spoken between us, and Su-Jin sang to us in the dark.

We made it to Mystic Lake, bypassing the campground and breaking into the patrol cabin. It was close and dusty inside. The odor of woodsmoke saturated our clothes, filling the room with its pungent aroma. I used what was left of my water to rinse the soot off my face one more time. After settling down for the night, I found myself lying awake wondering if we had gone far enough to escape the fire.

Dawn broke. The light that came through the cabin's single dirty window remained orange and eerie. Wind moved through the valley and creaked in the eaves overhead. I listened to Ford's quiet snores and realized Su-Jin was gone. Unwrapping myself from the sleeping bag, I crept to the window to look. The wind had changed direction in the night and thinned the smoke. Soot clogged my nose and throat. I needed to filter and refill my water despite the fatigue still clinging to me. I exited the cabin. The peaks above us were enclosed in smoke, the air clearer down by the lake where I spotted Su-Jin.

It was only a short distance to Mystic Lake. I brought my filter and stretched my sore arms and shoulders. I recalled passing through here in the summer and how it had looked then. The day had been clear, the jagged peaks of Mineral Mountain and the crumbling rocks of Old Desolate surrounded the subalpine lake. People were swimming in the water when I arrived, a couple of trail hikers enjoying a respite. Without hesitation, I stripped off my outer layers and joined them. The ice-cold water came as a sweet relief after hiking through the thick August heat.

In the present, smoke from the fire clouded and clung to those peaks. I had grown accustomed to Su-Jin's presence over the last two months. My anger had dissipated, and shame simmered in the background of my regard for her. She had warmed to me in return. Su-Jin had taken on a mothering role, pointing to the stick I was about to trip on or reminding me I was not drinking enough water. She still called me an asshole. I deserved no better, I had ended her life.

Sometimes, in the late hours of the night, when I lay awake wondering about the people I once knew and if they had survived, Su-Jin would sing. The song was haunted, visceral like a call to the other side, but her voice was sweet and lifted my spirit.

We were not friends. Our tentative connection was nothing like the demonstrations she made for Ford. She gravitated to him because he made her happy. He reminded her of someone she loved.

I sat on an old, petrified log next to the water. We admired the lake's surface, rippling as unseen insects broke the glassy plane. After a time, she sat down beside me. In profile, the angle hid her injuries. Over the months, her wounds had begun to heal. They were no longer open and raw; the bulging left eye had recessed. Only swelling and scars remained. It marred her otherwise perfect complexion. I was accustomed to seeing the damage and was momentarily taken aback to see her whole and perfect in this perspective. It was a long time before I spoke.

"Why are you here?" I asked.

"I came to see the lake," Su-Jin said, keeping her gaze ahead.

"No. I mean, after everything— At Sunrise—" I trailed off, looking down at my ash covered boots.

"I'm dead. Remember, asshole?" Su-Jin looked at me and rolled her eyes, a grotesque expression. I looked back out over the water and so did she. The haze in the treetops swirled with a gust of wind.

"Can we just talk?" I asked. She let the question hang in the air long before she replied.

"I have no answer. I don't know why you carry me," she said, "but that okay. I wouldn't see this without you." She indicated the lake with an uplifted hand. She fell quiet again. After a few moments, she said, "but I am ready to go. I want to. I miss my aduel, U-Jin."

"Your son?" I asked. I could understand her no matter what language she used, but I had learned I had to open myself to her to truly hear her words. When I resisted, it was foreign to me. I did not understand the language as if I could speak it. I simply knew the same way I knew she was Korean or that she was fifty-three years old. Or that she came to Washington on vacation, and she was unlucky to be here when the virus was released. I knew what her final days trapped in Sunrise were like. She never told me, but I knew.

Su-Jin had tried to survive. No different than what I was driven to do. It is impossible to have both anger and empathy. Knowing her terror lent itself to my shame. I understood why she did not ask for help and instead resorted to violence. It almost made my retaliation unfair, but it was survival. She had intended to kill me too.

"He was young," she said, speaking of her son. "But old enough to get in trouble. We lived close to the Nakdong. The boys would go swimming after classes when it was hot."

I could see the river in my mind's eye. A wide clear expanse, glassy and placid in its appearance, more like the lake we sat in front of than the swift current of a river. The water's edge was surrounded by lush trees and rich green grass. An elaborate bridge spanned its length with an ornate pagoda decorating its center. Young boys jumped from the bridge in their underwear, laughing and splashing each other as they tread water. Their clothing and bookbags scattered on the shore.

"It was deceptive," she said. "It look like it stand still, but it move fast. One day he didn't come home." Her eyes filled, and she quickly wiped away the tears before they spilled. I felt her as she recalled the officer arriving at her home to deliver the news, the piercing of her heart with grief and the wail of pure despair escaping her lips.

"He would be your age if he were alive. I have missed him for so long," Su-Jin said. "Ford remind me of him. Such a happy, sweet boy. You could not contain his spirit. Always on an adventure. Always smiling."

"I'm sorry you lost him so young. It's painful when they are young," I said, hesitating. "I lost my brother when I was sixteen." Bryce's face surfaced in my memory. His ruddy-brown hair with freckles smattering his nose and cheeks. His eyelashes were longer than most girls, and I had never missed an opportunity to tease him about it. He was forever frozen in time; he would always be twelve years old for me.

"I played hooky the day after I got my driver's license. I never missed school, but I was celebrating," I told her. "I was driving down some old backroads when my phone blew up. My friends were text-ing asking where I was, my parents were asking what was going on. The whole school district was on lockdown. 'A credible threat' was what my parents were hearing. The school had a way of being vague that always made things worse. As it turned out, they called it 'credible' because it was already happening. There was an active shooter at my brother's school. One of the teachers dumped her boyfriend, and the broken-hearted motherfucker decided to make her pay. I thought the police would evacuate the students, so I drove to the school to pick up Bryce. I didn't want him to be alone and scared."

"When I pulled up, I was surprised to see a perimeter around the building. The police had used the patrol cars and emergency vehicles to barricade the parking lot. All the emergency personnel were standing there, waiting. They were ready to go in, bags in hand, stretchers out, but no one was moving. Parents started arriving because we all had the same idea. A crowd was forming, and the police were holding them back."

"They never evacuated the school, in fact they did the opposite and tried to keep the parents from going in. It made no sense. They threatened to arrest people if they crossed the line. The parents were ready to explode. No one could understand why the police wouldn't go inside. It was maddening. If they weren't going to do anything, there were a few dozen moms and dads who would. It was getting out of hand when Bryce texted me. He said he was afraid."

I took a heavy breath. Waves of guilt and anguish flooded over me. I swallowed thickly and continued.

"I told him I was coming. And I tried. The parents were making a scene, and the cops were distracted trying to deal with them. I found a hole in the perimeter and slipped through when their backs were turned. I tried to get to him. I thought I could save him if I could get him out of there. Me. Only sixteen years old thinking I was invincible." I coughed out a laugh, but unrestrained tears fell from my eyes.

"They caught me halfway across the lawn. Shots came from inside the school when they tackled me. We all heard it. I could hear their screams as they pulled me away, and they still wouldn't go in. They weren't brave enough to get those kids, but we were. They stopped us from saving them. We weren't afraid. The heroes stood outside and let my brother die."

The officer who took me down stuck me in the back of a patrol car. I watched the SWAT team arrive, long after the gunfire stopped. It might have been minutes, but it felt like an eternity to me. When they finally went into the school, there was nothing to do except clean up the massacre. I didn't see the last message I received from Bryce until I was left in the car. It read:

HURRY

"Bryce was in her class. The teacher the man came to kill. He shot five students before he shot her and then himself. One of those kids was my brother."

I choked back a sob. Su-Jin was quiet, her eyes shut. I felt her beside me as the memories flooded in unbidden. Remembering my mother turning away from every emotion, refusing to process his murder to the point of being unable to look me in the eye. How my father, who felt everything in extreme, began drinking again after years of sobriety. My parents' divorce and their subsequent abandonment of me in those final years of my youth. Neither able to deal with me, a reminder of their loss.

"That is painful," Su-Jin said.

No more Saturday morning breakfasts with my baby brother, watching cartoons while our parents slept in. No baseball games with Bryce smiling broadly at the catch he made, dirt smudged across his freckled face. No more annoying little brother. No more best friend. This was the seed from which the fear grew. The worst thing that could have happened, did, and I lost everything. I froze in life the same way I froze on that bridge. While the current of time flowed past me, I stood still, unable to move forward.

"I'm sorry you are stuck here with me. I am sorry for everything, Su-Jin," I whispered. "I wish this had never happened."

Su-Jin replied, calm, "Peri, you are on an adventure. One here." She touched the center of her chest, the place over her heart. "We share pain, we share fear. I share this with you. It is as God wants it."

But the word she used was not God in her language or in mine. It was a bigger word, one my mind understood only by how the cacophony of senses felt: joy, pain, rapture, agony, exaltation, emptiness, and vastness. I was overwhelmed by it, but my heart was at peace.

"I think you understand better now," she was looking directly at me. "I would never be here without you. I am part of your journey. I would never see this place. You know, I crossed the world to come here. It was my dream. I am still experiencing my dream. It is a gift. I hope someday to see the snow. Not much snow where I grew up in Angdong."

"I will show you the snow," I told her, returning her gaze. Her wounds were gone and for the first time, Su-Jin smiled at me.

Our sights were set on Mowich Lake, but Cataract Valley would be as far as we made it before nightfall. Progress was slow. Even with both of us working together, it was difficult navigating obstacles on the trail with the wagon. The traditional Wonderland route crosses the Carbon River multiple times, so I suggested the Spray Park cutoff instead. Ford agreed. To get everything over the river would require emptying the wagon at each crossing and making several trips to bring over all the supplies. It would add hours despite being the 'easier' route in terms of elevation gain and loss. I was relieved. The Carbon flooded on a regular basis, and the bridges washed out often. There would be other river crossings after Mowich, but for now, I could postpone facing them.

The smoke lingered, but the direction of the wind helped with the air quality. The temperature was cooler today and the air heavy with moisture. I felt it against my skin. It made it easier to breathe. The sky grew thick with cloud cover hanging low over the trail, a strange mix of mist and smoke. The pungent woody scent of campfire punctuated the air.

Descending from Moraine Park into the Carbon Glacier valley, the path was a narrow, scree-covered cut into the cliffside overlooking the glacier's valley. It was barely wide enough to allow the wagon to pass. I strung a length of paracord through the under carriage and kept it taut in my hand to prevent the back end from sliding over the edge. Under the crust of muddy snow, rocks, and earth, it was hard to distinguish the glacier from the surrounding cliffs.

The Carbon's claim to fame was being the lowest elevation glacier in the lower forty-eight. I had hiked to this same overlook months earlier, an eighteen-mile round trip from the Carbon River entrance. The hike took all day. To reach the glacier, I traveled through an inland temperate rainforest full of gargantuan redwood trees. Over the years, some of these giants had collapsed under their massive weight and lay rotting on the forest floor, bringing forth new life. I stood as tall as their width, with centuries of rings to date their age. Moss and old man's beard hung from the branches and an endless sea of prehistoric ferns swayed gently in the cool air. The forest was lush and green. A beautiful sojourn through a less visited section of Mount Rainier National Park, and one we would not visit today.

When we came upon the suspension bridge marking the cutoff for the Spray Park Loop, we stopped to eat our lunch at the junction between the trails. We ate in silence, and I considered the history here before us. The glacier itself was a marvel in its size and scale, feeding the valleys below for miles from its muddy grey waters. A testament to the passage of time on this planet, it had carved out the valley before us and left the fields of talus below.

Dark grey clouds closed in around us, and the sky broke open and rain fell as we departed across the bridge. The trail beyond the bridge was marked only by infrequent cairns, scattered across the rock field. We stopped repeatedly to scan our surroundings, the fog concealing our direction. Our boots lost traction, struggling for purchase on wet rocks. The dirt became loose mud, and the sandy earth underneath gave way under our footfalls. The added weight and ungainliness of carrying the wagon between us made the passage unsafe and challenging, but we made it through unscathed.

Not every day on the trail is glorious. Some days are just hard. Today was like many in Western Washington: wet. I tried to keep up with Ford. Maintaining a steady pace, I put one foot in front of the other as misery leeched into my thoughts. Every muscle ached under the heavy weight of my bag. In Cataract Valley, we crammed our tent under the eaves of a large tree without much success. We would not be dry tonight.

When morning arrived, I remained in my sleeping bag unmoving. The dampness touched everything. Ford rustled around, leaning out the tent door to boil water. I stayed still, wanting to remain in my warm cocoon as long as I could, savoring the chance to rest. I was sore down to my bones. My feet ached. My pulse beat a tiny drum in the big toe of my right foot.

Ford offered me a cup of coffee, sensing I was awake. I sat up with immediate regret and drank from the aluminum cup still wrapped in my bag. After the coffee and a helping of oatmeal, I emerged into the world. We packed away our sleeping bags and pads then broke down the tent. I felt no eagerness to continue. I felt nothing but savage resistance to the effort it would require to reach our next destination. We continued because there was nothing to turn back to. Forward was the way home.

The continuous drizzle was broken up by occasional downpours. Ford whistled a tune I recognized, but the name of it eluded me. It was all I could do to redirect my thoughts from my own discomfort, so I focused on guessing the song. Reaching the meadows of Spray Park, autumn was in full swing. Between the shrubby subalpine firs grew vibrant golds, saturated maroons, and crisp reds replacing the once vibrant green ground cover. A doe crossed the path ahead of us, flicking her ears at the rain. Ford stopped, allowing her to pass. She hesitated, cautiously regarding us with her glassy black eyes, then went on her way. Su-Jin spoke to her in gentle tones. The doe looked back at Su-Jin, giving an eager wag of her tail, and appeared to bow before disappearing into the foliage.

The final mile into Mowich was a struggle. We were drenched and tired. The wagon got stuck on every obstacle. Wrenching it free over and over, my patience drained away. All I wanted to do was rest. Evacuating Sunrise had taken a lot out of me, my zeal for the trail eradicated by the labor of the journey. Ford's tenacity was a marvel. I envied his strength, his drive. He encouraged me to continue, maintaining positivity, so I pressed on.

Mowich feels secluded from the encroachment of the outside world. The road open from June to late October most seasons. For the rest of the year, it could only be accessed on foot. The park closed the gate at the boundary to prevent people from attempting the drive and getting stuck in heavy snow. The isolation makes it a quiet and rugged location.

When we arrived, everything dripped with the soft patter of rain. The clouds were low to the earth like they were held up by the tops of the trees, and the sky was pressing down upon us. Mist floated above the glassy plane of the lake like a specter. Only three cars sat in the parking lot. Drop by drop, the rainfall washed away the accumulation of tree duff and ash from their exteriors. I had the creeping sensation of being watched as soon as we came off the trail. The hair on the back of my neck stood on end. Ford came to a sudden stop.

The remnants of a yellow tent that had collapsed in on itself remained in a campsite. The sight of it unnerved me. Drawing closer, the poles were snapped and the material torn, in places shredded to ribbons. Wildfire ash coated the synthetic material. Rain pooled in the recesses, washing the soot away in rivulets and puddles.

Ford picked up a stick, using it to lift the rainfly. Underneath was the desiccated corpse of a man still encased in his sleeping bag. The down bag was ripped, and tiny fluffs of feathers caught the wind and floated away. The tent marked the man's grave. Ford laid the material down to leave him in peace and protect his body from the elements.

"Bears," Ford said, matter of fact. He pointed to a section of the rainfly with the end of the stick to show the strips torn by the claws of a curious animal.

"And there's the culprit," I said, pointing to a young black bear watching us by the pit toilets. Su-Jin gave a small gasp and stepped behind me. Ford looked first at the bear who watched us and then back at the claw marks on the tent.

"I don't think he's the one," Ford said. "I suspect his mother is. They must have figured out he was not good to eat." Ford took a moment to turn a full circle to take in our surroundings. He grew quiet, watching the shadows.

The bear was a yearling with fluffy reddish-brown fur. A bit of old man's beard and a collection of pine needles were woven in his coat. He was interested in us, evident by how he cocked his head like a dog, observing from where he stood.

"He's beautiful," I said.

"You won't want to meet his mother," Ford replied, hustling me toward the patrol cabin. It was a dark brown building built in the rustic park architecture found everywhere in the park. Thick ancient cobwebs hung from the eaves.

There was a padlock on the door, but the hasp looked weak. I attempted to shoulder the door in then gave it a couple of high kicks and found myself winded. Ford picked up a rock and smashed it against the hinge of the hasp. I turned away, my stomach flipping. Su-Jin did not react, her attention behind us on the yellow tent. She crossed herself, adopting Ford's habit, a gesture meant in compassion for the man who died here. The hinge gave way with a clatter. The metal dangled from the lock, and the door swung open.

After gaining entry to the cabin, I found a stockpile of kindling next to a relic of a wood stove. For the first time in weeks, we built a fire. Ford strung a clothing line across the room to hang our sodden clothes then draped the tent over a chair to help it air out. The cabin warmed, thawing my cold extremities. We pushed the wagon in front of the door to hold it closed. With dusk falling, I crawled into my sleeping bag without a meal and fell fast asleep.

It rained hard through the night, relenting just before dawn, and we woke to cleansed air. The trail caches, now months old, were stored in lockboxes with heavy lids next to the cabin steps. I found a can of root beer that was refreshingly cold. I drank it in long sips, the carbonation tingling against the roof of my mouth. Ford tore open a candy bar and took it down in three bites. We shared a freeze-dried breakfast hash to provide a bit more sustenance, and I won the single beef stroganoff meal in a vigorous bout of paper, rock, scissors. It was not only my favorite but Ford's. We found spoiled produce and something unrecognizable encased in blue fuzz in a vacuum sealed package. We took everything edible, managing to cram it into our bags and the wagon. We would have to withstand the additional weight.

We checked the cars left in the lot. While we dug through the trunks and glove boxes, I kept glancing over my shoulder, feeling an eerie presence, but when I turned to look, I found only trees. I guessed one vehicle belonged to our deceased man in the tent, the other two could have belonged to anybody. Ford said he had received a ride from a friend who hiked with him a short distance before turning back. The recollection dampened his mood. There was not much we could use. Ford took a couple of Washington road maps and a box of granola bars from the maroon pick-up truck. I found a pint of whiskey in the compact white car.

"All we need is a pack of smokes, and we could have ourselves a party," Ford chuckled when I showed him my find.

The mama bear appeared as we were preparing to depart. She was filled out from autumn foraging and eyed us warily. Black bears are ordinarily skittish and shy of people, but not this time of year and not when their cub is involved. She snorted a few times to warn us, pawing at the ground but not moving any closer.

"I am glad she is over there," Ford said. We started down the trail, and the bears, both mother and cub, tracked us a short distance then disappeared into the understory.

Leaving Mowich, the uncomfortable feeling quickly lifted. I had been on high alert during our short stay. The truth was it could have been the bears or the atmosphere but neither fit in my mind. I could not quite put my finger on the wrongness that set all my senses on edge, but whatever it was had frightened me.

We descended into dense forest. A downed log hung across the trail. It proved to be the first of many which turned our already slow momentum to a snail's pace. At each blowdown we lost time determining the best way to navigate around the fallen tree. I remembered a few from my circuit, but there were more now. I wondered how many years it would be before parts of the trail became impassable between landslides, washouts, and fallen trees. Without maintenance, how long before the trail would no longer exist at all?

At times the wagon fit under the fallen trees without issue and others, it had to be unpacked to some extent and repacked. Everything we carried was damp and filthy. When I began to question if the wagon was worth the trouble and wanted to abandon it altogether, the trail started to decline steadily without a single tree over it. One person could handle the wagon on the downgrade, so we took turns to give each other a break. For once, we covered ground at a pace reminiscent of our usual speed. It was not long before we reached the river.

We arrived at the North Mowich crossing late in the morning. The Mowich River was dangerous; the bridges regularly washed out during peak water flow and had to be replaced most years. The north crossing was the safer of the two, the expanse of this section was deep and narrow which made it less tumultuous than the south crossing. The south river was wide, and the water moved fast. It was notorious for the number of fatalities it had caused.

I breathed a sigh of relief when I saw the bridge was intact. Ford tested it, using his body weight to bounce the log to see if it was stable. When he decided it was safe, he crossed and emptied his pack. My heart raced.

The bridge was nothing more than a log. The handrail hammered into it seemed like a suggestion. It was there for stability; it might hold my weight, but based on how precariously it was attached, I suspected it would not. The muddy water roiled below.

Su-Jin crossed in front of me, unencumbered. I took a few deep breaths before stepping onto the bridge. I imagined it gave under my weight, for a split second the world swam, and I gripped the handrail hard. The vibration of the river came through the soles of my shoes.

I cleared my mind, listening to the blood rush in my ears. I took another step, mindful of the damp log beneath my feet. One foot in front of the other, I reached the other bank and remembered to breathe. Ford was done emptying his pack and ready to go back to bring food from the wagon. I fumbled with my buckles.

"Don't forget to unbuckle next time you cross," Ford reminded me. "You don't want to fight your bag if you go in, it will take you under." I nodded, feeling foolish I had forgotten.

"You did good," Su-Jin reassured me. I gave her a small smile and pulled things from my bag. The day was getting away from us, the shorter days becoming more evident as winter drew near. I felt compelled to move faster so we could reach our destination. The South Mowich River was less than a mile ahead. The next camp after that was Golden Lakes which was an additional seven miles. We would be lucky to make it before losing the light.

Ford and I each took turns bagging up our food supply and carrying it over. I would grow a bit more confident on each return trip, only to turn around with a backpack full and feel the familiar drop in my stomach watching the river's torrential path.

On my last crossing with a bag full, I froze only steps from the other side. Ford was watching, waiting to cross again and did not hesitate to reach out for my hand. I took it, jarred out of my inner world. It was like the river had stolen my mind. I was transfixed, my thoughts racing and unable to settle.

After several trips, we completed the task. Ford managed the wagon, lugging it over folded under one arm. I envied how easy he made it look.

It was only a short distance to the South Mowich crossing, and by the time we reached it, I was shaking. Instead of being reassured that the earlier crossing was successful, I was steeling myself for the next. My panic grew worse, and my mind flared with terror. The harder I worked to calm myself, the stronger my dread became.

Ford detached the bungees on the cart. We would execute the

same maneuver as the north crossing: breakdown the cache, make trips back and forth moving the food, then rebuild the wagon before our departure.

"Can you do it?" Ford asked with no hint of irritation in his voice. I nodded, exhaling slow and careful. He did not seem convinced.

"If you want to go across and wait, I can handle the rest," Ford said. I refused.

"It will slow us down if you work alone," I said. Ford accepted my response then crossed the bridge to unpack his bag on the other side.

I did not tell him how much I wanted to overcome my crippling anxiety. I had kept hoping it would get easier, but I no longer believed exposure to my phobia would help me outgrow it. No matter how many times I navigated across the rivers in the park, it always threatened to lock me. The only choice I had left was to refuse to let it rule me and learn how to coexist. I chose to accept the fear.

The river was high from the rain. South Mowich was a wider expanse than the north crossing and prone to washouts. Many lives had been lost here. Although still in place, the center of the footbridge was bowed, the log curving into the river. It was almost fully submerged, the rapids had crested its middle point and flowed over the top. The water was the brown of chocolate milk, frothing and violent.

"Is it safe?" I yelled across the water to Ford. He cupped a hand to his ear over the roar of the river.

"What?" he yelled back.

"Is it safe?" I yelled again, pointing to the portion of the bridge below the water's surface. He gave a thumbs up.

I stepped onto the bridge, unsure. The handrail felt flimsy under my palm. The pounding water made me dizzy and unstable. The log under my boots was wet and slippery. I felt it flex and vibrate. I willed my feet to move. One cautious step at a time. I got to the bank on the opposite side and with shaking hands, emptied my gear. Ford patted my shoulder.

"You are doing great, kid," he said. I watched him cross back over, wishing for the confidence and ease in how he moved.

I unloaded, taking slow, steady drags of air and willed my heart to stop racing. I crossed back, relieved without the weight. My stomach clenched and my head swam, but before I knew it, I had stepped off into the sand where the wagon remained. I took items from our supply and put them into my pack.

Su-Jin was there, silent. I sensed her anxiety, recalling the memory of her son.

"I'm okay," I said to her. Ford looked up at me, confused. Su-Jin said nothing. She watched me work for a second then crossed to the other side.

After loading my bag with a portion of our food cache, I stood and looked across the bridge to where Su-Jin waited.

"It'll be over before you know it. You can do this," I told myself, psyching myself up. My body wanted to lock in and freeze. Ford had finished filling his bag. He swung it over his shoulders and crossed nimble and quick, his hand barely grazing the rail as he went.

Without thinking, I clipped my waist belt and stepped onto the South Mowich footbridge. I moved fast, feeling a slight rise in my confidence as I imitated Ford's light footfalls, when the bridge jerked. It shifted under the pressure of the current beating against it, jolting beneath my feet. I missed my next step. My fingers slipped. I flailed, attempting to grasp the handrail at the last second. As I dropped my wrist smashed against the log, and I was submerged in the freezing glacial river.

My mind had no time to register the fall before I was under. I held my breath and soon surfaced, gasping, to see the speed at which I was being pulled downstream. For a split second, I saw Ford and Su-Jin picking their way across the stones along the riverbank before I hit a boulder and was thrown into a faster current. The water was like ice, my constricted lungs inhaled short bursts.

I pointed my feet downstream to ride the current, like I once had as a girl, hoping my legs would absorb any impact. A snag under the surface sliced through my calf. It stung for a split-second, my extremities growing numb. I could not feel the gash. I grasped for an overhead branch, missed, and went under again as the river gained depth, the weight of my backpack dragging me under water.

I fought against the buckle of my hip belt with cold, feeling-less fingers. I could not unclasp it, the belt tight against my body. I smashed into a large boulder. For a second, as I was forced against the rock, I was able to drag myself out of the water and suck in a lungful of air.

I did not know if I could hang on until Ford arrived. They were too far upstream. Two tiny distant people racing along the river. I gripped the boulder for purchase, but it was slimy and wet with no fingerholds, and I kept slipping. Water pressed me into the stone. Feeling myself begin to slip, I reached higher to pull myself out. The stream grabbed my bag, heavy and saturated, its weight shifted, and I was sucked downstream.

The current held me. With my pack full of water, it was an anchor holding me down. I fought to keep my head above the water. A large branch stabbed into my ribs. The pain was immediate, searing through my torso, and I lost all focus. My body recoiled into itself, no longer able to tread water.

I went under again; my arms and legs were numb. I had no more fight in me. I held the last of my air despite the urgent pressure to release. Bubbles drifted from my nostrils as I leaked my last gasp. Water filled my lungs.

This is death, I thought, growing calm. The glacial current held me in its grip. The burning in my chest, the need for oxygen, was subsiding. I gave in. I accepted its embrace. I was going to die. The moment felt suspended outside of time. No cold. No pain. I was at peace, surrounded by a dark, comforting warmth. A light dawned. I reached for it.

Unseen hands hoisted me out, and I was dragged onto the river-bank. I sputtered, coughing up dirty river water and half of my last meal. When I looked up, Su-Jin stood there soaked. She was breath-ing hard.

"You forgot to unbuckle your pack," Su-Jin said. "Asshole." She unsnapped the belt and wrenched the soaking bag off my body. For a moment, I thought she was angry. I was disoriented and exhausted. I rolled onto my back looking up at the grey sky gratefully sucking air.

"You okay?" Su-Jin asked. She wept silent tears. I reached for her, and she took my hand.

"Thank you," I rasped. "Thank you. Thank you. Thank you." She squeezed my hand. It felt warm in mine. My breathing slowed. I shivered uncontrollably.

"Oh, thank God, Peri," Ford exclaimed, dashing up to us. He knelt beside me and took me into his arms, wrapping me in his body warmth.

"I thought I had lost you," he said, his relief unmistakable.

"You won't get off that easy," I replied through chattering teeth. He smiled.

"You were lucky, but we aren't out of the woods yet," he told me. He reached across to my saturated backpack, checking several pockets before digging out the waterproof matches. He gathered a few small twigs. On his second attempt, he maintained a flame. He fed the fire, bit by bit, generating a plume of smoke from the wet wood. When the fire could withstand him walking away, Ford moved me as close as he could and left me alone while he collected my gear. Su-Jin stayed by my side.

He came back with a dry outfit and my sleeping bag. I was cold down to the core of my bones. The fire soothed me but did little to ease my shivering. Ford helped me remove my soaking clothes, turning his head away as I stripped off my undergarments. I was unabashed, desperate to get warm again. Ford wrapped my sleeping bag around me, zipping it up to my chin. I lay down next to the fire.

He warmed water on one of the stoves, poured it into my water bottle and placed it into my sleeping bag with me. I felt Su-Jin at my back. She moved in close and placed a hand on me. I was reassured by her presence. Ford kept talking to me, waking me each time I drowsed.

"You can't sleep yet. You need to drink something warm," Ford said. He handed me a cup of coffee that I tried to refuse. I was annoyed, wanting to sleep, but I drank the coffee. Ford built the fire higher. The deep chill I felt began to release, and I could feel my feet again. I do not recall when I gave into sleep.

I awoke sometime in the night to find Ford awake, keeping vigil over me and the fire. We were prone, and it was a lucky break the rain had held. Ford had surrounded us with our supplies, having brought everything over the river alone while I slept by the fire.

"I couldn't keep you awake," he said. "I have been watching you breathe all night. How are you feeling?"

"Could be better," I replied. I ached all over. The deep scratch in my calf burned. The left side of my ribcage felt as if an ice pick had been stabbed through it. Each breath was painful. I hoped it was not a broken a rib. He encouraged me to get more rest and I did.

In the morning, Ford made me a bowl of oatmeal and gave me one of the painkillers from the bottle we found in the RV. We reviewed my injuries, and Ford wrapped a compression bandage around my chest to help with the swelling. Most of the food I had been carrying was damaged or lost, scattered along the riverbed.

Ford wanted me to rest, but I insisted we move on.

"There's a patrol cabin at Golden Lakes. We are exposed here," I reminded him. "The weather won't hold for long."

"Are you kidding? You almost drowned, you were borderline hypothermic, and you might have a broken rib or two. I'm not sure you realize the climb we have out of here. We'll be fine another day, I can get the tent set up," he said. "If you are worried about exposure, we can cross back over the river to the camp." The oxycodone and ibuprofen had worked their way into my bloodstream. I felt impatient and eager to get away from the river.

"I feel good actually," I lied. Ford eyed me as he packed away the stove then shook his head.

"First of all, bullshit with this 'I feel good'. I don't buy it. Second, you won't be able to help me with the wagon, and I can't carry your bag too. If we go today, your backpack is your problem, and I won't hear a word about it," he told me. I scowled at him and agreed, remaining stubborn to the end.

From our location to Golden Lakes the trail climbed nearly 3000'. The switchbacks felt never-ending. I realized too late I should have listened to Ford's objections. Every time I looked up, the trail rose away, the pinnacle unseen above us. Ford slogged up the mountain, slowly rolling the wagon. The pace was painstaking and slow, yet I trailed behind him, relying on two found sticks as trekking poles. I used them to steady myself, each lungful of air I took was pure agony.

I had overestimated my ability to continue, especially after the injury to my chest. The ache radiated through the opiate fog. Without the medication, I had no doubt I would not be upright, let alone climbing a mountain. I felt every pound of weight in my pack that day. The trail eventually leveled out, the last couple miles gently rolling into Golden Lakes. It was a sweet relief.

We arrived at the cabin, Ford started a fire, and I went to sleep. The next morning, Ford checked my injuries a second time, concerned I had made them worse. The deep slice in my calf had reopened while trekking out of South Mowich, evidenced by the trickle of dried blood down my leg, but had crusted over with an ugly scab. I had various minor cuts and bruises all over my body. My wrist was swollen from hitting the footbridge as I went down. The worst of all was the purple and black discoloration on my rib cage.

"If they were broken, I don't think you would be moving at all. We certainly would not have made it here," Ford admitted to me. He rewrapped the compression bandage. I winced each time he pulled it tight against the bruise.

"It's going to be a few weeks at least before you get back to normal," he told me. I nodded, defeated. Ford insisted we would stay in the cabin until I could carry my backpack without the aid of the poles. I accepted it, no longer willing to fight him.

We stayed in the cabin five days. On the sixth, I told Ford I was ready to move on to Longmire and the following morning, we did.

Leaving the protection of the cabin, the rain began again in earnest. We reached the first Puyallup crossing by the afternoon. The river was unseen, but its familiar chorus rose as we approached. I felt nothing except the nagging pain in my side.

Ford turned down the spur trail for the individual camp sites. I continued onto the boardwalk, my footfalls clunking along the wood path. The dense foliage opened to the footbridge, and I stepped onto it, finding myself in the center before realizing where I was.

My pulse did not quicken, my breathing steady. My mind was clear and able to admire the landscape around me, the gentle rapids below cascading over slate-colored boulders. The sun sank below the cloud cover and filled the valley with warm light, igniting the surrounding forest and reflecting off each raindrop.

Su-Jin and Ford appeared at the entrance to the bridge. Ford's surprise was written across his face. Su-Jin graced me with a big, beautiful smile.

My fear was gone.

Soaking in the moment, I felt free. My worst fear had been realized, and I had survived. I laughed, turned, and finished crossing to the other side.

We stayed in the North Puyallup campsites that night and the following day we moved onto the South Puyallup Camp. Again, I crossed the river without hesitation.

The following morning, we climbed to the top of Emerald Ridge along a cliff face overlooking the Puyallup Glacier. I helped Ford manage the wagon, carrying it between us. It was painful for me, but I managed. The sky remained overcast with occasional showers. The meadow at the top, a verdant green in mid-Summer, reflected the rich colors of an autumn palette.

The descent from the ridge led into a moonscape. The sweeping meadow disappeared, transitioning into the carved valleys and peaks the Tahoma Glacier had cut centuries ago. Ahead of us, a wall of crumbling andesite surrounded by stone fields. The mountain was hidden from view, but the edge of the glacier could be seen above the deep oranges and greys of the surrounding cliff faces where the receding ice had ground away and exposed the layers of earth. The valley was vast and unearthly. Mount Rainier's name before white settlers arrived was Tahoma meaning 'Mother of Waters'. Given the number and size of the glaciers on the mountain, it is not hard to understand why.

The trail passed from dense forest filled with moss-covered trees to an open field with an endless sky to a crumbling cliffside overlooking the glacial river valley below. It was nothing short of astonishing with or without the mountain in full view. We continued until we reached Indian Henry's Hunting Grounds and slept in another patrol cabin. It was evening when we arrived. The clouds had parted, and the sun appeared, exposing the previously hidden mountain view. Su-Jin and I admired it side by side.

After my fall in the river, Su-Jin's injuries, including the semi-healed scars, vanished. All signs of our struggle were gone. She was perfect again, made whole once more. Su-Jin beamed at me, a bright aura surrounding her as she looked up at Rainier.

Su-Jin had pulled me from the river when I had nothing left within myself to fight. Her strength had surrounded and protected me. Somehow her act had released me from my paralysis, and I was not sure I deserved the gift she had given me. I had overcome my fear.

The sun began to set behind us. Alpenglow lit the mountain. The clouds were on fire with golden sunlight. Su-Jin smiled, turning in a slow circle to take it all in. She laughed out loud, embracing the moment with a fullness that took my breath away. We were caught in a singularity. It would exist only now. I was present here and full of all things.

Under the shadow of a volcano, I found a wonderland.

"It'll be easier to drag that thing on the road," I said, annoyed, pointing at the wagon. We had reached the road through Longmire. One direction would take us there, and the other continued on to Paradise.

I was depleted. In truth, we were both exhausted from our days on the trail. Ford barely showed it, but I could see in how his shoulders slumped, fatigue was setting in.

Since we left South Mowich, Ford had been primarily responsible for the wagon. I helped when I could, but carrying my backpack was all the demand my recovering body could handle. My bruised ribs made it painful to breathe. I was grateful for the narcotics. I could not have continued without them, but I was ready to be done depending on pills. I felt guilty relying on Ford to shoulder the burden, but he accepted the responsibility with no complaint. Between the rain, my injuries, and the weight we carried between us, the journey had taken its toll.

"We should stay on the trail," Ford said. "We don't know what we will find. We need to be careful." He was carrying the gun in the open. Locked into my mind, consumed with pain and misery, I had not noticed that he had retrieved it from his bag. He was right. I adjusted my attitude, pulled myself out of my own head, and followed Ford back onto the trail.

The rain had let up, but the day was grey and gloomy for late morning. We reentered the darkness of the understory. A stillness hung in the air as we approached Longmire. The forest made no sound; our feet, and the wagon too loud by comparison. A building appeared on our left through the trees. A simple brown lodge blended into the shadows.

"Let's clear this building and stash our things. We can check the rest unencumbered," Ford said. He looked keyed up and I felt it too. He added, "I expect this will take the rest of the day, but I don't want to be caught off guard if someone is here."

This was the plan we had discussed as we headed south on the Wonderland. Our priority would be to ensure we were safe, which meant determining if other people were in residence at Longmire. If we found we were not alone, we had to decide how we would handle it. We agreed we would try diplomacy first, and if that failed, we would find somewhere else we could stay long term. Violence was a last resort. I had no desire to relive Sunrise, but knew if push came to shove, we could not afford to hesitate.

Ford went inside to clear the building while I waited outside, guarding myself with the hatchet. Su-Jin furrowed her brow, observing the increase in our stress levels. Ford had warned me about what we were walking into while I healed in Golden Lakes, sharing the experience he had long with-held. One night, as I lay on my sleeping bag in the patrol cabin, unable to sleep due to the pain but unwilling to take anything stronger than ibuprofen, I heard Ford sigh next to me.

"Are you awake?" I had asked.

"Unfortunately," he replied. I could hear the tone in his voice.

"What's wrong?"

"I'm worried about Longmire. Worried about people," he said. I propped myself up on my side and regretted it immediately, returning to my back. Ford heard me rustling around and rolled himself over to look at me.

"Tell me what happened," I said.

"I ran. I hid," he replied. "I could have done more, and I did nothing."

"Knowing you, Ford, you had to," I said. "Tell me what happened."

"After I left Mowich, the trail and campgrounds were quiet, which I thought was strange. I saw a few people but not many," he said. "I had no sense of what was happening when I arrived in Longmire, but the virus was sweeping through." He hesitated before proceeding with the next part.

"I was getting my cache and noticed a hiker, a young guy, approaching a man who was getting into his vehicle to leave. The second man didn't even hesitate, pointed a gun, and pulled the trigger. Now I understand he got too close. I wanted to help him. The man with the gun was watching me, to see what I was going to do. He had the gun ready, it looked like he would shoot me if I came any closer. I ducked behind the building, and he hopped in his truck and burnt rubber out of there."

"I started to walk over to help the hiker who'd been shot when I saw someone else on the ground. They were leaning up against the bathroom, propped up. I was too far away to tell, but there was blood pouring from her eyes and nose. Her head was at an unnatural angle, and I realized she was dead. At first, I thought she had been shot, then I realized there were others, all around me in similar states. The blood, the bruised skin. I grabbed my bucket, and I got the hell out of there. I waited until I was back in the woods before I emptied it," he said. "Cougar Rock was the same. Bodies everywhere, people had abandoned their camp except there was one tent, and someone inside was calling for help. He kept saying 'I don't want to die' over and over. I didn't stop. I didn't ask if he needed help. I walked away. I kept moving."

Ford rolled over onto his back and covered his face with the crook of his elbow.

"I should have helped them. I think about it all the time. I should have done something," he said.

"You are human, you know?"

His voice grew choked, struggling with words.

"Abandoning someone when they need help is inhuman," he replied.

I rolled over, despite the pain, and wrapped my arm around him.

"You didn't abandon me," I reminded him. His body racked with quiet tears, after a time he calmed, and we both fell asleep.

I reflected on what he had shared as I waited. The sadness Ford felt at what he believed was a failure and my immense gratitude he had survived his experience. Like me, he had made the choice to survive, but there was no escaping the consequences inherent with that decision. I believed it made him more human.

"So much death here," Su-Jin said, interrupting my thoughts. She stared into the forest. Through the trees were other cabins, and beyond those the central buildings of Longmire.

"Maybe you should wait here," I said, her anxiety increasing my own. She nodded. When Ford exited and gave the nod for all clear, we hid the cart and packs inside, then continued into the woods. Su-Jin watched us go from the porch. I wondered if it was a mistake to leave her behind.

We came to another road. Through the woods was a parking lot and a scattered array of buildings. I was shocked. Months had passed since the initial event, and what was left behind still took my breath away. It was as bad as Ford said.

Compared to Sunrise, Longmire was a graveyard. There were

a dozen or more abandoned cars. Broken safety glass littered the ground like tiny blue diamonds spilled across the pavement. The bodies were long into decomposition after laying out for months in the heat and weather. They were nothing more than husks wrapped in a shroud of dried blackened skin. There were skeletons picked apart, bones scattered. The animals had sorted the sick corpses from the healthy. A human rib bone lay less than a hundred feet in front of me, white and picked clean. It disturbed me. The cold autumn air held no odor, and for that, I was grateful. Ford made a pained face.

"It's alright," I said. "We can go back to the cabin and do this tomorrow." My ribs ached, and I half-hoped Ford would agree so I could rest. I needed to rest. Ford shook his head.

"I need to know we are safe," he replied. He stepped into the lot, over the loose rib, coming in behind the Wilderness Information Center. He climbed onto the porch waving for me to follow. I was already overwhelmed by the number of buildings to clear.

The entrance at Longmire was open year-round. Before Rainier became a national park, Longmire was a health resort utilizing the mineral springs scattered throughout the area. It was named after the homesteader who once owned it. After the original resort was demolished, the National Park Inn was built to memorialize it. In addition to the larger administrative buildings serving as park offices, there were numerous living quarters, single room cabins and chalets, set back into the forest. The maintenance area was a fenced off gravel lot, built with modern garages and storage units to hold the equipment and plows used to maintain the road to Paradise in winter. Last, the pride of Longmire. The collection of historic rustic lodge style buildings forming the heart of the site: the Wilderness Information Center, the old gas station and museum, and the National Park Inn, which included both a restaurant and a general store. An American flag still waved at the tent pole.

We explored the maze of buildings in silence, clearing each area to verify our solitude. A countless number of people had succumbed to the virus here, revealing the speed in which it moved, killing people before they could leave, some even as they packed their bags. The virus had arrived with someone, and wreaked havoc on those it came into contact with. Others had met with premature demise, which I could deduce based on the evidence of animal activity. It was devastating. Why people had chosen to kill each other was a mystery. Even though I had firsthand knowledge, this was something else entirely. The chaos and terror were evident.

Silence persisted. We moved onto the Longmire General Store, a lofty title for the gift shop adjacent to the National Park Inn. After clearing the inn, which had taken a while given the number of rooms and closets to check. We had been through the Wilderness Information Center and museum prior to that. I was tired of looking at room after empty room, body after dead body.

Between the inn and the store, beneath the covered walkway, were the remains of a child. I stopped, staring at the tiny frame wondering who had abandoned her and left her to die alone. A crash came from the store ahead. Ford lifted the firearm to chest height and took slow, cautious steps toward the entrance.

"Ford," I whispered, "stop." I gripped the hatchet as I passed in front of the darkened shop's window. Ford pulled the door open on quiet hinges, and we listened. There was only silence. He indicated for me to hold the door. I did as requested, and Ford went inside.

The room was dimly lit, the late autumn light low in the afternoon. Ford moved through the shelves on silent feet. As my eyes adjusted, the rows of coffee mugs and piles of shirts took shape. A few items had been knocked to the floor. Ford was careful to step around them. A sound came from the back room, the door hanging ajar into what appeared to be a storage area. Ford misplaced his step, kicking what sounded like a ceramic mug across the wooden floor. It rolled heavily, loud against the quiet. Another clatter came from the back room.

Ford froze. I came fully inside the store with my weapon across my chest and walked to the door. Placing my hand on the knob, I locked eyes with Ford. He came behind me, gun at the ready, I swung the door open, and Ford pointed the weapon in.

We were met with a hiss from the biggest raccoon I had ever seen.

He flattened himself in a defensive posture. I relaxed my arm. The critter was raiding what was left of a box of candy bars pulled down from a shelf. Boxes and souvenirs littered the floor. It was clearly not the first time he had visited this room. His ears flexed and turned as he watched both of us still holding the chocolate in his tiny paws. We each stepped back, and I went to open the building's front door. The critter scrambled outside, carrying his prize.

We surveyed the mess, finding a lot of the food had been consumed or disturbed by the animals. They had gained access to the building through a broken window. I laughed out of relief, but my ribs seized.

"It was mostly gifts and candy," I offered.

"I will take whatever calories I can when it comes down to it," Ford replied. We had quickly surveyed the inn's kitchen. We would not be relying on what we brought from Sunrise alone, but at first glance, it was less than what we hoped for.

We cleared the rest of the buildings, found more signs of animal activity in a few of the bunks, and too many dead bodies to count. As we uncovered each one, the weight of it pressed on me. When we resolved we were the only living souls in Longmire, except for some curious wildlife, we returned to the first cabin where Su-Jin waited. I found her sitting on the porch, and she stood on our arrival when she saw the utter dejection on our faces.

To think, we were the lucky ones.

The National Park Inn became our home for the winter. Ford busied himself inventorying supplies as soon as we moved in. I suspected he did it as a way to distract himself from our surroundings. He started with the kitchen of the inn's restaurant to better assess our food situation. After that, he surveyed the outer buildings one at a time.

October transitioned into November and overnight, temperatures dropped below freezing. It felt like fall had shown up and left just as quickly. It was surprisingly sudden, like the cold had held off in time for our arrival. I was grateful it did.

I took up residence in one of the first-floor parlors of the inn with a large stone façade fireplace to continue my recovery. There were rooms upstairs with actual beds, but I sought the comfort the hearth offered. Some of the rooms were unusable. People who died in their beds, or as they packed, remained. Until we could remove the bodies, Ford closed them in and placed an 'X' on the door with some duct tape he had found.

Most of my minor cuts and bruises had healed. My ribs continued to ache, but it had become tolerable. The only thing for me to do was rest and allow them to mend. So, I rested. Ford gave me a blanket from one of the upstairs rooms. I wrapped myself in the musty fragrance of it and watched the flames dance in the fireplace. It was a relief to know we would not have to pack up and leave again. We could stay.

Su-Jin sat with me, staring out the window into the forest. She had grown distant after my white-water adventure. There was a sadness in her, but her thoughts were closed off to me. I was concerned but too exhausted to give it more attention.

Ford checked in on me. He added a few logs to the fire, gave it a quick stir, and then left to get to his chores. I settled in with a thin paperback with yellowing pages. The book had lived here so long its cover was permeated with the smell of woodsmoke. It was a mystery, and while I was not a fan of the genre, it was the closest thing at hand to occupy me. A few chapters in, the heat from the fire seeped into my bones. It felt good to be warm, and I drifted off to sleep.

When I woke, the fire had burned down to red-hot embers. Su-Jin had abandoned her post at the window, and I was alone. My mouth was dry, and my head felt stuffed full of cotton. I had wasted a good chunk of the morning napping. I wandered into the kitchen where Ford had brought in a bucket of fresh water and filled my bottle. Padding through the main lobby on my return trip, the front desk caught my eye. A bit more awake, I went into the cubby behind the ornate counter. When I found it, I knew it was what I had been looking for.

I found a fragment of a newspaper from the Seattle Sun-Times, only a couple of typed sheets, and realized the two pages were the entirety of what had been printed. It contained no ads or pictures, only copy and a lot of blank space. The headline spanning the top read "We May Not Survive This." It was a single article, typed in a large font to fill the pages. It was printed the day I came through Longmire last August, and it was about the virus. Two days later, Ford would be confronted with the horror of this new reality.

It opened with a demand letter of an environmental group named Mother's Garden. I had a vague memory of hearing the term but did not know the source. Print media was dead to my generation, no one read the paper anymore. I had stopped consuming television news, and often scrolled past social media pertaining to current events. The rhetoric was designed to incite, not inform.

The article first provided some background. Detailing how in 2029, Mother's Garden had forwarded their statement to the White House, the Pentagon, and every senator and congressperson, along with an assortment of U.S. government offices. Additionally, it had been sent to the UN and leadership of the other 195 countries who had signed the 2015 Paris Agreement. News outlets had been made aware, but the story was relegated to the back page, focusing more on the group's controversial history than the warning itself. The government would not substantiate the threat, and it fell off the public's radar.

Mother's Garden demanded that the President, as the leader of the civilized world, and the UN take immediate action to adhere to and enforce the Paris Climate Agreement. The environmental group contended that many of the countries, including America, were not delivering on the pledge to reach a fifty percent reduction of greenhouse gases by 2030 and would not meet the deadline due to wasteful spending and a lack of enforcement. In particular, it referenced the "utter failure" of America's 2022 Inflation Reduction Act meant to provide greater funding towards the effort. Similar subsequent legislation in the EU, Canada, Argentina, and China were panned as ineffective at best and destructive at worst.

Mother's Garden claimed they were left with no other option: since the world's nations would do nothing, the planet would require cleansing to save it. There was no other way to preserve Earth, the only home for humanity. It cited suffering all over the world due to drought and the monopoly on clean drinking water by American corporations whose profits reached the billions. It criticized the super wealthy for their focus on vanity projects, sending man into space over investing in a concerted effort to resolve world hunger or global warming. The singular investment of one billionaire could have changed the course of climate change decades ago. It went on to provide examples of the many failures: train crashes spilling toxic chemicals into waterways, the destruction of honeybees around the world, and Fukushima to name a few. The only thing vague about Mother's Garden statement was how they would execute retribution for noncompliance. If their ultimatum was not met, they would act. A list of specific requirements followed.

The known history of Mother's Garden was limited. They were considered a low-level terrorist cell masquerading as an environmental group with fanatical cult-like tendencies. Its members were linked to self-immolations on the steps of the Supreme Court and sabotaging oil rigs and pipeline development. The FBI had trouble tracking the group because they were decentralized, with no specific leader and no central location. A few individuals had been identified: a leading scientist in his field, a college student only nineteen, and a single mother of two, but there was no unifying body, connection, or common ground between the members. It left more questions than answers.

As it would turn out, the threat had been real all along. The article reported the Pentagon had confirmed the theft of a classified virus from a BSL-4 maximum containment facility in early 2030 but only announced it to the public once they were able to confirm that cases of Ebola were appearing in a Portland hospital. An informant asserted that when the virus was stolen earlier in the year, the CDC and the WHO had set the greatest minds all over the world to the task of developing a vaccine in secrecy. The CDC claimed they were unclear if the virus had been misplaced or stolen, but they acted on precaution by working to produce a vaccine. Breakthroughs in technology and medicine led to hopes it could be done.

Governments did little to nothing to address Mother's Garden's ultimatum.

After its release, Mother's Garden claimed responsibility. Their announcement was followed by a rash of suicides attributed to the group's members, filmed on individual social media accounts, although this was largely overshadowed by the problem of the budding pandemic.

The world's governments watched and acted in the hopes of outrunning the virus. The WHO issued a global 'Do Not Travel' mandate. Each country reported various stages of closing their borders and shutting down air travel. Both Mexico and Canada were shooting US citizens on sight who attempted to cross into their countries.

The CDC issued an imminent warning of the highest level. It advised everyone to shelter in place until further notice. The President placed an executive order grounding all planes leaving the United States. Every person was allowed twenty-four hours to find shelter in the hopes of waiting out the virus. The result was chaos. The country made a run on the grocery stores. The homeless were shot dead in the streets. Home invasions were rampant. It was all too late.

The American government failed to raise the alarm despite knowing the 'missing' virus would likely trigger an extinction level event. Survival rates were placed no better than five percent. The statistics were so dire, there was no mention of setting up field hospitals or emergency services. No information was offered about how the virus would be responded to. A contagion so virulent, aid was not even being offered in order to limit the spread.

I had come of age under the dark auspices of climate change. The dire warning was impactful, leading to a generation of children disenfranchised by the systems that allowed global warming to continue unabated despite all evidence. It was hard to ignore our environmental impact. Billions of pounds of plastic entered the ocean each year. The growing hole in the ozone. More than ten thousand species threatened with extinction at any given time. The seasons of my adulthood barely resembled those of my youth. Fires came every year, significant glacial mass had been lost in the northern hemisphere, and storms had increased in severity and size, wreaking havoc on communities across the country. Extreme weather became the norm. Hurricanes destroyed whole cities and tsunamis leveled islands. In parts of the world, deforestation and desertification had become so significant that all arable land was gone, limiting the food supply in poorer countries. Richer nations were like a glutton at the dinner table, consuming beyond their need, and yet many of their citizens were no better off than those in a third world country. Humanity chose to squander its most precious gift: Earth.

The article simply ended, reading more like a list of statements strung together than a cohesive report. Based on the typographical errors I found littered through the text, I suspected the print had been rushed. I believed I was holding one of the last newspapers ever released. No conclusions were drawn or stated. The article closed with a farewell from the author and that he loved his daughter.

Reading about the disaster after all this time was strangely disorienting. How long did they make it out there? What was left of society outside of our bubble? A deep sadness washed over me, and something else too. It was relief. We were the cancer, and the virus was the cure. The terrorists saved the planet by killing us, and I felt no outrage, only a deep and abiding pain that it had to come to this. Mother's Garden was the end of us, and also, the true savior of Mother Earth. She would survive, and maybe, we could start again. I read the article again. And then again.

My energy was depleted after the third readthrough. Any hope that had remained was gone. I had confirmation: we were the last of us. There was horror in this discovery. Something I had suspected but could never fully believe. I had a new perspective, and an unknown world lay before us. How long would we last? I returned to the parlor and sat in front of the fire, wrapping myself in the blanket again. Ford found me there hours later, staring into the flames.

On a morning, in the midst of my convalescence, I woke to laughter outside. I went to the window out of alarm, the glass condensed with moisture and radiating the cold from outside. Wiping away the fog to look out into the cool morning light, I found Su-Jin twirling outside in softly falling snow. I watched tiny puffs of white dance around the small woman, crystalline flakes landing in her jet-black hair. Su-Jin was radiant in this pure moment. She looked like a five-year-old on Christmas morning with a crown of snowflakes. Our eyes met, and she smiled.

"Snow!" she exclaimed. I laughed with her. Her excitement reminded me of winter mornings with Bryce. How he would wake me, full of delight at seeing a blanket of fresh snow on the ground. We would dig out our snow boots from the back of the closet, pull on our jackets, and go outside to play. When we came in, we would shed our soaked clothes, have a hot cup of cocoa and a snack, and wrap ourselves back in the wet outerwear to play until dark.

The first snowfall brought back that childlike sense of wonder. I felt the urge to join her. I was ready to get back outside, and Ford could use my help preparing for winter.

As if my musings had beckoned him, Ford appeared and joined me at the window to watch the snow fall. He smiled the wide grin that overtook his whole face. For a moment, I believed he could see Su-Jin too, catching snowflakes on her tongue. I wished he could.

"I was coming to tell you it was snowing," Ford said. He had been hanging blankets over some of the windows to help insulate the inn. The size and age of the building would make it difficult to heat through the colder months, and it would help conserve our firewood supply to not have cold air leaks.

The snow fell for a time then transitioned into rain once the day warmed. What had stuck to the grass and pavement was washed away. Our time before winter had reached zero.

We woke to clear skies a week later. I was ready to get moving again, in fact, my body was practically demanding it. Bad weather would keep us inside plenty of days through the winter months and far fewer would be nice enough to hike. We did not hesitate to take advantage.

Ford said he wanted to show me one of the best views of the Cascades, so we embarked to Van Trump Park, which would also take us past Comet Falls. We picked up the Wonderland for a mile until a squat wooden sign appeared with an arrow pointing the direction of the falls.

Winter hiking is a more involved experience, requiring extra supplies and additional planning to account for all conditions. I felt bulky and hot under the weight of my added layers and hefty pack. Aside from the residual ache in my chest, my ribs seemed to have healed, but I felt deconditioned. The trail itself skirted a valley carved by the Van Trump Creek. It was a steady climb; one I was not prepared for. As if reading my mind, Ford spoke up.

"You are stronger than you give yourself credit for, Peri. Stop doubting yourself," he said over his shoulder, the cold air freezing his breath. I smiled, grateful for his confidence in me.

We reached the snow line, and the ground disappeared under a blanket of powder, thin at first, but growing heavier as we ascended. The higher we went in elevation, the more precarious the trail became as the whiteness obscured the line of the path. I felt dizzy in sections where the grade slid sharply away into the creek.

Su-Jin walked between us, almost on top of the snow like a red fox hunting its prey. The lilac fleece and grey slacks were sparse apparel for an icy winter morning, but the chill did not slow her down. Her cheeks were roses of color on milky white skin. They framed a brilliant, bright smile. Her deep black hair shimmered in the sun, reflecting the blue sheen of the snow. Her aura was luminous.

The sun rose over the mountain and shone into the valley. We were warmed by its rays and began shedding our outer layers. From time to time, we stopped to clear the ice balls as they accumulated on the chains of our microspikes. I used the opportunity to bask in the sunshine. It was a beautiful day for a hike. The trees wore coats of fluffy snow. Animal tracks crossed and dotted the untouched trail. The network of rabbit, fox, and deer were visible between the maze of trees. I spotted a set that I believed to be a bobcat. Ford insisted it was a young fox. We argued playfully with each other about who was right.

Comet Falls appeared in the distance as we crested another rise. Su-Jin stopped to admire it, and I came up beside her, so we stood shoulder to shoulder. Her smile grew, crinkling her face with plea-sure. I had never been here before. It was a happy moment to share this first with Su-Jin. We were joined by our awe.

"Wow," I breathed, taking it in.

"Like the tail of a comet, right?" Ford laughed.

The three of us continued forward, navigating the trail and the creek on our approach. Mist rose from the base of the falls, filling the valley with moisture. Drops had frozen on the surrounding trees and rocks forming an ice garden. Stalactites of ice glistened from stone faces, and droplets of water formed where the sun hit. Water poured over the cliffside like the streaking tail of a falling star. It reminded me of the meteorites crossing the sky at Fremont Lookout. I took it all in: the sound, the smell of moisture and moss underneath the ice, the white-blue snow blanketing the earth, the sharp cold touch on my face. We stayed here in quiet meditation for a short while, enjoying a snack until we grew cold and moved on.

"Final push," Ford said, slouching his pack over his shoulders. The incline to Van Trump after the falls was steep. My ribs ached. The frigid air burned my lungs with the effort it took to attain our final destination.

"Most people only hike the falls. They don't know what they are missing," Ford said. "The park is named after P.B. Van Trump, one of the first men to ascend Mount Rainier. Christine Falls was named after his daughter. He was an interesting man. It's said that the first time he laid eyes on the mountain he knew he would climb to the top someday. And he did. He worked on behalf of the park in different capacities well into old age. I admired him for that. I considered volunteering with the park too."

"Why didn't you?" I asked.

"I was intimidated," Ford replied. "Everyone was so young. I didn't think I would fit in. By then the website kept me busy."

"Well, they would have been lucky to have you," I said.

Ford smiled, continuing to make easy chatter while moving up the vertical climb. I gritted my teeth and saved my air. My calves burned. I was drenched in sweat. My mind shifted into a lower gear, tuning in to the movement of my body and taking one step after another.

We arrived at the junction. The top of Tahoma was visible over the ridgeline. From here the incline eased up, and my breathing steadied. When Rainier came into full view, the volcano towered above us, and it was glorious. Rainier's glaciers were full and white, shining in the reflection of the sun. There was not a single cloud in the sky. The snow-covered meadow of the park stretched out around us. I made a full turn to take in the expanse before me. Mount Adams stood prominent in the distance, and Mount Saint Helens beside it, the crater of its deformed face visible. Far on the horizon sat the ghost of Mount Hood rising out of the blue. It felt like the crown of the world.

"I just—" I trailed off, unable to collect a single thought, captivated by the far-reaching views. The joy between the three of us was palpable. Su-Jin was ecstatic. She glowed, like a switch inside of her had been flipped. All at once, I realized what was happening. There was a long silence as she took in the beauty before her.

"It's time, Peri," she said, a serene smile on her face.

"No," I replied. I resisted her, and a wave of sadness threatened to swallow me. I fought it, but all the mixed feelings I had held for so long released and crashed upon me simultaneously. I swam through the tide of my many conflicting emotions. Happiness. Despair. Fear. Shame. Peace. Time froze. Tears welled in my eyes, and I surrendered.

"Please don't go. I need you." I began to cry. Unbidden memories washed over me. The face of my brother. My first backpacking trip, standing incapacitated over the Greenwater River. The bloody stone in my hand. The realization I had stolen a life. For a flash of a second, the rock lay between us in the snow, splashes of crimson on my hands. Su-Jin's head collapsed in on itself, her wounds reopened, and her life force flared out. It was like killing her again.

Then the vision was gone, and Su-Jin was herself again. Sobs shook through me.

"Time to let that go, you ready," she told me, covering my hands in hers. "You don't need to carry me with you any longer." Her presence burnt so bright I was blinded, and then the light began to fade. Su-Jin faded with it.

"I am ready," she said. "I have seen so many beautiful things because you held me within you. There is nothing to be afraid of anymore. It's time." Tears poured down my cheeks and froze in the cold air. She smiled.

"How do I forgive myself for this?" I asked her. She stroked my cheek.

"I have. You should too," she said. I grasped desperately for her hands as they vanished. I wanted to hang onto her and keep her with me. I could feel her leaving, like the universe pulled her out of existence. Her absence a vacuum in me. She was gone.

A deep pain welled inside of me then released. What I had been holding and resisting since the moment I had crested the hill at Sunrise. What I had suppressed after that final message from my brother. The hurt, and the fear of what those moments meant. Trying to comprehend the incomprehensible: the shame of surviving when others were lost and the responsibility mine to bear. So, I carried them with me to remember, my regret becoming my greatest burden. I had surrounded myself with the dead and wondered why I had chosen not to live.

Su-Jin was gone. I stood there, numb. Empty. But there was something, a tiny radiant center in my chest warming my heart. My tears stopped, and I felt the rush of exaltation. A small light that was mine.

"That's strange," Ford said. "I lost a moment there. You look like you've seen a ghost." I had forgotten he was there. I turned away from him, wiping my damp face. He understood something in me had changed.

"This is a spiritual place, Peri. Some people say it's a thin place between this reality and the next. I have seen things in the shadow of this mountain I cannot explain. Things where they should not be. Things that make no sense to the rational mind. The natives believed powerful spirits guarded this mountain. I tend to agree with them," Ford said.

I nodded. "Ford, there was a woman in Sunrise. I never told you. She attacked me when I came off the trail."

Ford's surprise was evident. I continued, "I fought back, and I killed her. I didn't mean for it to happen. I've been carrying this horrible thing I did around with me. I'm so ashamed. I killed her! She's dead because of me!"

I gasped for air as sobs racked my body, the tears starting again in a torrent. Ford stood still for a split second then showed his unconditional and immediate acceptance of me by wrapping me in a hug.

"Oh, Peri," he said, his voice sad. His warm embrace reassured me, and I felt that small light grow. After a while, Ford smoothed my hair back and placed a kiss on my forehead. He kept his arm around me, and we stood together marveling at how far we had come.

I **went forward** without the existence and constant reminder of Su-Jin. I missed her. I had grown so accustomed to her presence and the shame I felt, it had become a part of me. Ford once told me: "Sometimes the comfort of our pain is easier to withstand than the discomfort of our growth." He was right.

I was unable to accept the life I had taken, no matter how justifiable. What had transpired between Su-Jin and I was inevitable. Our paths had been set to cross. Nothing I could have done would have changed it, then or now. Instead, I carried her memory with me, and I held it with absolute love. I said a prayer for her every morning when I woke. I was mindful I had taken her life and lived because of it. I owed her a debt, and in my heart and mind, I repaid her by making amends every morning. I survived by the grace of her death.

I never returned to Van Trump Park.

Where Sunrise was desolate and removed, Longmire reminded me of civilization. It ushered in a nostalgia for life before the virus. I missed things like curling up under a blanket to binge watch a television show. The plots from programs I used to follow would pop into my mind at random moments, and I would wonder how the stories would have ended. I missed the internet and how the answer to every question was available at my fingertips. I fantasized about turning on a faucet and sitting under a stream of hot water until it ran cold. I regularly returned to a well-worn memory of a fine restaurant where I was served a perfectly grilled steak, a baked potato with all the fixings, and a green salad. I missed the convenience of my former life. Before the virus, I had romanticized the alternative. Now that dream was reality, and I found myself with the total freedom I had longed for.

I came into adulthood at a time when buying a home had become a fairy tale I was told as a child. I envied the people who broke new ground looking for other routes to economic solvency: the homesteaders, the builders of tiny off-grid cabins, the van-lifers. The simplicity of it appealed to me. I never took the risk. It looked like freedom from the outside looking in, but I was unable to let go of the stability and safety I had created. The freedom I had today was total, but it came at a price. Freedom is not free, it demands sacrifice.

Thanksgiving arrived and brought with it the storm of the century. We woke up to several inches of snow and dark angry clouds. Looking out the windows was like watching a television broadcasting static. The drifts grew, covering the cars, trees, and surrounding buildings. It purified the landscape and concealed the ugliness the virus left behind. The inches became feet with no sign of stopping, so we brought in enough firewood to remain indoors for the duration.

Ford used the time to take a hard look at our food situation. It was apparent our supply would not last us the winter. What had been lost to the river was inconsequential, but it was a loss just the same.

We had checked out all the buildings and vehicles in Longmire and found less than expected. The kitchen supported a fully functioning restaurant. Since the pandemic hit at the height of summer, the pantry stock had been depleted. The inn could have been expecting a delivery. All the fresh items had long since spoiled. The Longmire system was hooked into the main power grid; no solar panels or batteries to keep things running here. Neither of us were willing to see what food borne illnesses the walk-in cooler contained. We were lucky the property had a working hand pump to get fresh water.

Ford began a project. He calculated our caloric intake versus our output, factoring in less physical activity in the winter but also giving allowances for activities like chopping firewood and hiking. He reviewed the calories in every item we had, splitting our intake over three meals a day. On his first run through, he calculated thirty-three days' worth of meals for the two of us.

Time became inconsequential cooped up in the inn. The hours unspooled in front of me and slowed to a trickle. I found a few books to read, avoiding the plentiful collection of romance novels I found. An employee of the inn must have been an ardent fan of bodice rippers, there was hardly a bookshelf where they did not dominate. But even as an avid reader, I could only spend so many hours with my head bent toward a book.

I was a restless explorer faced with never-ending winter. Only the second day into the storm I was full of nervous energy. Out of boredom, I tried to nap, laying down in front of the fireplace expecting to doze the afternoon away. Instead, I found myself conscious again after a short time in that dreamy state just below the surface of waking. It did nothing to help pass the time.

Ford, on the other hand, was a solitude specialist. It was obvious he relished his time alone. He wrote in his journal. He dozed by the fire. He read. Ford was wholly unperturbed by the time spinning out in front of him.

I spent periods in those long hours remembering what my life was like before the virus. I lamented the time I had wasted, the time I spent not truly living. It was difficult to accept. To avoid and mitigate risk, I had chosen a path out of fear. There is no growth without pain, and I made decisions to avoid discomfort. How much time had I thrown away? When I chose to embrace risk and to challenge my fears, I found real happiness, true joy, and contentment. Even now, amidst what could be the worst experience of my life, I had found serenity.

During our time inside, I saw a side of Ford that illuminated who he had once been. In his past life, he had grown a business adjacent to the tech industry when tech was soaring high. Given his early retirement age, the amount of free time he had, and the quality of the clothing and backpacking gear he used, I knew his line of work had been a successful one. Ford was both meticulous in his accounting and shrewd. He thought he could improve upon the first result, so he ran the numbers again. He cut down on our daily consumption which added another week and a half. This time, it allowed us forty-four days. Ford went back to the drawing board again, still unsatisfied with the outcome.

The man I knew of shining smiles and endless positivity was changed while he set his mind on this project. This version of him was ardent, driven, and focused. Ford cut our intake further. It left no more room to maneuver if we followed the rigid plan he had laid out. It gave us fifty-one days.

After the revelation about our food, I fought the temptation to become a hedonist and give in to all my impulses in response to the hopelessness of our situation. I fantasized about eating like a king, exploring the outdoors when the weather cleared, and then dying here in front of the fireplace. I recognized our plan to remain in the park was, in some way, already submitting to that compulsion. We planned to return to the trail as soon as we could, prioritizing hiking over survival. The lack of resources would throw a wrench in our plan. We either had to find a solution or leave the park before the end of winter.

"Fifty-one fucking days," I muttered, flipping through the pages of handwritten numbers. The nights were long, and the wind outside howled. It made strange, haunted sounds in the eaves of the old inn and rattled the single pane windows in their frames.

We sat by the fireplace, the pint of whiskey and a deck of cards between us on the coffee table. I had brought the cards out for a game of Spades. Ford had appeared with the whiskey along with his findings. He explained his conclusions to me as he poured a knock into two ceramic mugs.

"Unless we want to ration well below a maintenance intake. That's already the bare minimum," Ford replied. "We could add more time, but all we would be doing is prolonging the inevitable. That road won't be pretty." He emphasized this by giving me a serious look. I took his meaning. We would only be alive in the literal sense.

"We could garden," I said weakly. It was a lame suggestion. Ford shook his head, sipping from his mug.

"Have you seen what it looks like outside?" he said, pouring another. "Never mind we have nothing to work with, no seeds or starts."

"I found a book about the forest flora. Do you know anything about edible plants or mushrooms?" I asked. The book was old. It had a section about foraging, but the pictures were simple line drawings and descriptions.

"That one you showed me? Well, that's a great way to get poisoned. I know a few things, but I also know that most plants look like other plants that will kill you. What about hunting?" Ford replied.

"With what? The handgun? We have six bullets," I said. I fingered my mug and sniffed the liquor.

"I know," Ford sighed. "My dad used to take me hunting when I was little. We don't have a rifle so big game is out of the question. Not like I am a good shot. But he did show me how to set snares for rabbits and break them down. After the storm, we'll be able to find the prey trails. I can teach you how to skin a rabbit although I am rusty."

I grimaced and slumped on the couch. The thought of having to kill a small animal made my stomach turn. I drank my whiskey down and held out my cup for more. Ford saw my face and poured another shot in.

"We can cook them over the fire, it would be good to have fresh food," Ford said.

I continued to stare at him. I was sick of processed food, but it was food. I was not convinced I was capable of skinning bunnies.

"I found a fishing pole and a small tackle box in one of the cabins," I offered, already knowing it was not fishing season. We would be lucky to catch anything more than a snag.

"It's not the season," Ford echoed my thoughts. "When this bad weather clears, we should go to Paradise. There was a restaurant and a gift shop there too. There should be some kind of stock or supply."

"Honestly, it's not too far for us to go to Ashford and see if the grocers have anything left," I responded. Once began, this conversation had a circular way of coming back around to the same points over and over. I had suggested this before, and the response was always the same. Ford leveled a gaze at me.

"As much as you don't want to skin rabbits, I don't think Ashford is a good idea. It's too risky. We have no idea what it's like out there," Ford said.

"What if no one is out there? We've already cleaned out two restaurants in the park. We aren't going to find as much as you think we will. I'm sure of it. Paradise is going to look the same as here," I argued. "I think we can find more in Ashford. A lot more."

"By the spring and summer, we might have some luck fishing. I think there are apple trees around here somewhere," Ford said, avoiding the subject of Ashford by taking another sip of whiskey.

"Look, if we want to stay here, we'll have to figure it out. I think it's inevitable. Eventually we'll have to leave," I replied.

It was hard to be firm making decisions with so many unknown factors. We had resolved to stay in the park without fully acknowledging what it would require. I wanted to spend the best months back on the trail. Ford did too, but we had to face the reality that the fun and games would not last forever.

The conversation fell off and died. It always ended up at the same conclusion. We would have to leave some day. I watched the flames and considered where to go next.

After a while, Ford picked up the deck of cards, and we started a game.

"What about the Pacific Crest Trail?" I spoke. The alcohol had worked into my bloodstream, leaving me uninhibited.

"What about it?" Ford asked.

"What if when we leave here, we hike the PCT?"

Ford gave me a surprised look.

"We don't have enough to stay here. What makes you think we will last on a longer trail?"

"Hear me out," I said. "There won't be many people. I am sure we will encounter some, but if they are hiking the PCT, we can hope they will be like us. There is a benefit of heading south. If this winter has already shown us anything, we want to be somewhere temperate. There are towns along the way, I think most are pretty small, where we can resupply. There will be houses too. Maybe we could stay in one. We won't be right in the thick of it, in a city. We could make a home somewhere, at least for a little while."

Ford stared at his cards then set them face down on the table.

"Peri," he said, "I want you to know I could have never survived this without your friendship."

"Ford, I—"

"I'm not trying to be overly sentimental but let me say this. All my life I have felt different, separate. In some ways, I was. I am. I tried for a long time to fit in. As a teenager it was playing football and hunting with my dad. As a young man, it looked like marrying a good woman. It took me years to see I loved her in a way, not like a husband should love a wife, but she was a wonderful person. In truth, I don't think I knew real love until my sons were born, but your children are meant to outgrow you and mine did. All those years, I threw myself into work and building something because I believed that was my purpose. But I always felt alone. I had friends, community, a family, but I didn't belong anywhere."

"I have had a good life, I never felt true connection. I think it is a human need to be understood by another, and it always felt like it was just out of my reach. I would go through these episodes of utter despair, wishing I had one person who could see me for who I am. Maybe the problem is I never showed anyone who I truly was. You won't find people if you don't show yourself. I hid behind my work and the happy family façade. My wife knew, she always knew, and she cut me loose. Not because she was unhappy, because she knew I wasn't, and I needed to go find what I was looking for."

"I started the Wonderland website hoping to find like-minded people to connect to, and I did, but it turned out to be surface level. It was the same as everything else. It became like my career, something to hide behind. The only time I felt at peace was when I was alone out here on the trail. I belonged here. Then I met you, and we were the same. Tell me, Peri, have you ever felt like you truly belonged?"

Unexpectedly, his words hit a nerve in me, curdling my mood like spoiled milk. It was a sentiment I was all too familiar with. My nose stung, and I suppressed long-held tears. Ford was describing what lived in the darkest recesses of my heart: the deep loneliness and all-encompassing bouts of depression that had pervaded my existence. I knew the truth; I had never belonged anywhere.

"No," I said. I folded my arms around me, trying to close myself off from the ache inside my heart.

"I know you see me because I see you. What happened in your life disconnected you from others. It changed you. I felt that way too, until we met. I was grateful to find anyone left alive here. I could have managed on my own when it came to the survival stuff, but the stuff up here—" He tapped his temple. "I don't know. I am glad it was you."

"I will go where you go. We will go together, but I am not willing to take unnecessary risks. I don't think I could live with myself if something happened to you. I don't think I could bear it. You are my best friend."

"I'm your only friend," I sniffed, but smiled. He laughed then. He poured more whiskey into both of our cups and raised his in a toast.

"To Peri: my only friend," he announced. We both laughed, clinking our mugs together.

"I am glad it was you, and I'm happy you are here with me. I believe we were meant to find each other here at world's end. More than anything, I'm grateful you found me," I said, reaching out and squeezing one of his hands.

We finished the pint and played cards until we were too drunk and too tired to continue. People spend so much time looking for love, favoring the romantic type above all else. Every person hopes to find true connection in their lifetime. I found it in a friend. Ford was my family now. Ford was home.

The rabbits were easy to find, it was snaring them that proved to be difficult. The weather had abated for a time, leaving a slate grey sky and a fresh layer of snowfall covering the ground. We donned our winter gear and headed out into the woods.

"Wherever there are blackberries, there are rabbits," Ford told me as we stepped through ankle deep snow, scanning the ground for prints. A single deer had crossed the forest floor earlier this morning. Ford regarded the tracks, pausing for a moment, and continued through the blanket of snow. When I spotted the first rabbit trail, I laughed. There's no denying that rabbit prints in the snow look phallic; from the weight being placed heavily on the back paws, to the length of the animal's body.

"I will never not find it funny," I told Ford as we approached the dense underbrush of blackberry shrubs. "It looks like a tiny penis and balls hopped through the snow." I laughed.

"Thank you for the imagery, Peri," Ford remained serious. Attempts had been made to cut back the blackberries to prevent them from encroaching. It was a futile effort. Some of the vines had grown long without intervention.

"I know, I know, it's not very refined of me," I said, ducking under one thorny arm.

"Nothing wrong with finding humor in things," Ford said, crouching down in the snow next to a trail of rabbit tracks. Their prints were fresh and many. Ford pointed at the imprints.

"This is exactly what we are looking for. We can set a snare here, I'll show you," he said. Ford had sourced a heavy gauge wire from a toolbox on one of the maintenance trucks. He took a length of it from the roll he carried, snipping it off with a set of pliers that materialized from his pocket. Ford used the nose of the pliers to hold the wire as he wrapped one end to form a loop. He showed me how it would slide along its own length to close around the rabbit's neck. He wrapped the other end of the wire around the base of the tree, which was a small fir about a finger length in thickness and tied it off a few inches above the ground.

"You get to make the next one. It's important to block around the snare. You want that loop to be the open path, so they choose it," Ford said. He broke a couple of low hanging branches full of pine needles and arranged them around the noose. Ford had me build the next snare. I worked slowly, wrapping the wire around itself, unskilled with the technique.

"I am not good at this," I told him, clumsily wrapping the wire.

"That's okay. I haven't done this in a long time," he said as he collected branches.

"That isn't how it looked to me, seemed like you had a good handle on it," I replied. Ford shrugged.

"Muscle memory, I guess," he said. "Sometimes the hands know what the brain doesn't." We set a few snares like the first. As we moved into denser forest, Ford found a vine maple he liked the look of.

"I am going to show you how to set a spring pull. It requires a little more effort, but the benefit is that it will get the rabbit off the ground away from predators," Ford said. He took the hatchet, skinning the sapling of its branches. Ford dug around and found a thicker branch below the snow. He chopped a length as long as his forearm then used the back of the tool to hammer it into the ground.

"This is the anchor." He indicated. Next, he chopped a finger length chunk off the same branch and wrapped the noose around it. Ford cut an angled notch into each piece with the knife then lined them up, so they hooked together. I watched, careful to remember each step, huffing puffs of cold air and swaying from side to side to stay warm. When he was satisfied after a few adjustments it would hold, he pulled a fold of paracord from his pocket.

"Now we tie this chunk with the snare to the vine maple. When the snare goes off, the tree will yank it upward," Ford told me. He cut a length, then tied the smaller piece of branch to the maple, bending the sapling and hooking the small section to the anchor by fitting their notches together. He used the last portion of branch to set the snare off which yanked the wire loop into the air.

"See?" Ford said, looking over at me. "Eventually this maple won't have as much spring, but it will work for the time being."

"You weren't kidding, that one requires a lot more work," I said. He nodded.

"It'll be worth it if it keeps another animal from eating our catch. Let's see if we can find you one to set up. It won't hurt to have a few of these around, and I think you should know how to do this. You might need it someday," he said.

"That's why I have you," I joked. Ford made a face, a flash of an expression. A frown. We walked the perimeter of the blackberry patch, searching for another ideal spot for the next pull snare.

"What's with the face?" I asked.

"What face?" Ford replied.

"You made a face, just now, and you're being a grouch today," I said, growing annoyed with his feigned ignorance. We had grown so close to each other sometimes I was unclear where he stopped, and I began. It was like mind reading, something was bothering him. Ford had been prickly all morning. He was covering it by focusing on our task, but it was troubling him. I had not noticed at first, assuming he was tired like I was. He remained silent.

"Ford!" I shot him a look that said 'what gives'? He shook his head.

"I had a bad dream last night," he said. He would not look at me as he spoke, "It got to me. I can't get it out of my head."

"Well, are you going to share?" I asked.

"We were on a trail in this dense forest. The trees were these colossal, oversized things that towered into the sky so high you couldn't see their tops. They blocked all light from reaching the forest floor. The trees were wrong though, like I was looking at the legs of some massive unseen animal, and we were tiny insects trying to avoid being crushed. It was like the nightmares I had as a boy. This heavy mist moved between the trunks like it was this living, breathing thing. We couldn't see anything ahead or around us, but there was this bright white animal coming toward us. When she became material, I could see it was a doe with these huge black eyes. She was pure white and almost shining despite the darkness. She didn't startle or run away. In fact, she came directly up to you with her ears forward, so you held out your hand. She rested her head in your palm and cried. But not tears: blood, blood poured from her eyes." Ford shook his head as if to get the image out of his mind. "Then I woke up." He grew quiet again.

"The trail. Blood from the eyes. The forest. All of that sounds like pieces of our present reality sewn together. You must be stressed about the food situation. Besides, don't dreams always mean the opposite of what you think they mean?" I tried to reassure him, but the disclosure left me unsettled. Ford's response to this dream seemed out of character, which made me worry.

"For me," he said, "it think it means something bad is coming."

Names carry meaning, and many of the places in Mount Rainier are aptly titled based on what they embody. Wonderland is one. Paradise is another.

Ford and I followed a network of trails past Narada Falls north to Paradise. The waterfall was charming, the river flowing over the rock carapace like white strands of hair, cascading over every step. We did not stay long, the best way to stay warm on a frosty day is to keep moving. Over our heads the sky was open and clear, but dark grey clouds threatened the lowlands. The bank of clouds formed a wall extending for miles. Whatever pressure system the mountain created held the impending weather at bay.

My microspikes cut through the frozen ground, providing satisfying crunches with the weight of each step. The snow grew denser. The higher we went, the whiter the scenery became. Animals had broken trail for us in places, in others there was only the slightest indentation in the drifts to indicate we were where we should be.

Reaching the top, the south face of Tahoma filled the entire horizon. This view of the mountain was both different and the same from the one I grew up looking at each day. Rainier was beautiful from every angle, but I marveled at how depending on the perspective, the view was entirely unique. The south had similar traits, new patterns, glaciers, and peaks to learn, but the volcano's north face was imprinted in my mind as home.

Arriving in Paradise stirred a memory, one that surfaced from the forgotten places of my childhood. It was summer. My mother woke us early, piling my brother and I into the car with snacks and our blankets. We fell back asleep during the long drive. Waking as we arrived at the mountaintop, the coolness of morning was fading, the sun shined, and the hillside was an absolute riot of wildflowers. Bright sunny yellows, vibrant pinks and purples swayed in the gentle breeze. My mother had dressed me in a light blue summer dress with white polka dots, the fabric thin and comfortable for a hot day. I recalled the vastness of the mountain, immense and beautiful, creating a backdrop against the cerulean blue sky. Our mother had brought us here for a picnic to enjoy the scenery.

Bryce was only a toddler. As much as she tried to keep him from picking the wildflowers, the moment my mother turned her back, Bryce would pluck them from the meadows. He collected a small bouquet by late afternoon. Returning home, my mother showed me how to enclose the flowers in folded sheets of wax paper and press them between the pages of a heavy book to preserve them. That book was filled with four leaf clovers she had saved and the bud from every arrangement my father had ever brought home, including one from her wedding bouquet. A history in blooms.

"This used to be a golf course," Ford said. "Could you imagine?" His cheeks were flushed from the cold.

"That's some bourgeois bullshit," I replied.

"They used to ski here too," he said. "Eventually they figured out they were destroying the meadows, put an end to all the recreational activities, and cut out a trail system. That was when they built the Skyline Trail."

We crossed the parking lot, weaving around vehicles encased in ice, tombs for frozen bodies. Did they come here to take in one last beautiful thing before they died? Did they know it was the end? They were part of the strange landscape of this disaster. Snow covered everything here. The Paradise Inn and Visitor Center stood like dark monoliths against the surrounding white sea, their first levels half-buried by the drifts. We waded through with some difficulty, managing to navigate despite the moderate snow level.

The Paradise Inn's dramatic roof, steep and two stories high, rose above us, the structure tucked into the back of the lot. Only the inn's top story was visible from our approach. Built into the side of the slope, the lower floors were buried into the hillside which made the inn's size and scale imperceptible. The Annex, built later to accommodate more guests, was visible in the valley below. Additional supports were placed to bear the weight of winter at this elevation. Snow had drifted against the building's main entrance, piling high and burying the wall of windows with no one to remove it. Only the top of each window was visible.

"I guess I didn't consider this. Do we break a window? Dig it out?" Ford asked. "All I have is my cathole trowel or an aluminum cup."

"I'm going to look around, maybe there's another way in," I replied. The ground sloped away from the entrance on either side of the building. First looking down one side, I saw no exterior doors, no balconies, and no windows that could be used as an access point. Walking back past the front of the building, I shook my head at Ford.

"Nothing over there," I said. He grimaced. On the opposite side, I noted the odd way the snow piled against this corner of the building. Snow had sloughed off the roof, piling higher in this one section, burying something at my chest level underneath the layer. A balcony.

"Ford!" I called. "What is in the building on this corner?" He considered.

"Pretty sure that's the restaurant and dining area. I don't come up to this part of the park often," he replied. I walked down the slope into the deepening snow and found myself waist high when I spotted it. Behind the wall of snow, there was a tiny alcove invisible from the building front. In it was a bright orange bucket placed under an eave where a cluster of icicles had formed. They dripped steadily on its frozen surface. At the back of the alcove was a door.

"Ford!" I yelled. He appeared above me. "I think we can get in through here."

The outlines of the balcony and railing were evident from this angle. I did not want to attempt to go through the wall of snow. What remained on the roof would slide off and bury us if we broke through it.

"Can you help me up?" I asked him. Ford waded down, folded his hands, laced his fingers together, and cradled them for me at knee level to use as a step. Feeling into the snow to find the structure under-neath, I braced myself against the balcony railing and placed my foot in Ford's folded hand. When I stepped up, I searched for the top rail, blundered, and lost my precarious balance. I tipped backwards, the powder making a soft *wuft* as I landed on my back.

"Are you okay?" Ford asked. A gleam of suppressed laughter in his eyes. I lay sprawled, staring at the sky, contemplating if I felt any-thing more than mild embarrassment. Giggles bubbled out of me. I shot a thumbs up straight into the air. Ford let himself go, cackling with amusement.

"Good. That looked painful," he wheezed. I laid there with the coldness enveloping me, enjoying the pleasure of contagious laugh-ter. When our chuckles subsided, I waded out of the drift with some effort. We knocked snow off the balcony until it was visible and wound up nearly buried in a heap of white dust. Ford helped me up a second time. I clung to the side of the railing, placing my feet, and swinging my leg over the top. Once on the platform, I held my hand over the side to Ford, who grabbed it and replicated my maneuver onto the balcony.

Through the alcove was a door, and behind the door was the interior of the inn in darkness. The orange bucket was an odd feature, frozen solid and spilling over with water. The pool around it was a sheet of ice. I shuffled by, careful not to slip.

"What do you think that is?" I asked Ford, pointing at the bright container. I stepped into the alcove, tried the door, and found it swung open.

"Peri!" Ford said sharply. "Hang on! Someone might be in there." I let the door close, relieved to know we could access the building. The sky was beginning to grow dark, and we were not prepared to sleep rough. Ford cupped his gloved hands against the glass and peered inside. After a moment, he pulled back with a deep sigh. He indicated at the bucket.

"It looks like someone was collecting water," he said.

"Who knows how long that's been there. We'll be careful," I replied. I opened the door again. We entered, cautious. As Ford guessed, the door opened into a large semi-formal dining area. Dried muddy footprints led into the building's interior across the hardwood floor.

I took a moment to sit in one of the chairs to remove my microspikes. Ford did the same. The rubber around my boot was chilled and did not want to release. After a few moments of struggling, I pulled one off and then the other. It was cold inside; my breath coming out in faint puffs.

We weaved through the log tables and chairs, tracing our way into the main lobby. The floor transitioned from hardwood to a rich burgundy carpet. The ceiling soared away, and a massive chandelier of antlers formed the centerpiece of the vast airy space. Floor to ceiling log poles framed the structure and despite the temperature of the interior, the building felt warm. We walked past the windows of the front entrance and the bell desk to reach to the opposite side of the floor.

It was a cozy space. A massive stone fireplace dominated the back wall with several overstuffed leather sofas and chairs with large ottomans surrounding it. A velvet rope cordoned off an old piano placed in front of a window with a breathtaking view of Mount Rainier. A lump of blankets lay on the floor in front of the bare hearth. At first glance, they seemed out of place until I realized there was a man wrapped inside them. I stopped. Ford peered past me.

"Hello?" I called.

"My God," Ford whispered. I did not need to look to feel Ford cross himself behind me. No response. I took another couple steps forward.

"Do you need help?" I offered, my voice echoing in the cavernous space. No response, and no movement came from the man.

"He's dead," Ford said. We crossed the floor to where the man rested. It was obvious he had died recently; decomposition had hardly touched him. There were no streaks of blood from his eyes and ears or mottled skin. If it were not for the faint blue cast, he could have been asleep. The temperature in the building was only a degree or two warmer than outside. The chilled air had preserved him. I was not prepared to find a corpse like this. All evidence indicated this man had survived.

It was apparent the inn was his home. There was the bed made up in front of the fireplace with a stack of books and a glass of water next to it. Those were his muddy footprints at the side entrance, and the bucket appeared to be part of a catchment system for water, collecting water from drips and snowfall. Split wood was piled high beside the fireplace.

"No worry about that running out," I said, admiring how well the firewood was stacked. It must have taken quite a while to get it all in here. Each fit together like pieces of a puzzle.

"He didn't die from the cold." Ford observed.

Another person had endured the end of mankind. How long

did he last? His cheekbones stuck out like sharp edges. His eyes were sunken into the deep sockets of his skull. I was relieved they were mercifully shut. He was emaciated.

"He starved," Ford said, standing over the man's body. "He's too thin."

"Or it was a heart attack. Could be an electrolyte imbalance," I replied. Ford and I locked eyes, the realization dawning on both of us at the same time.

"There's no food here," I said. Ford's eyes grew wide. He dumped his bag on a sofa and returned to the dining room on the other side of the floor.

"Ford!" I yelled as he hurried away. He did not stop. I followed, not wanting to be left alone with the corpse. When I caught up to him, he was already in the restaurant's kitchen casting about in vain. The open shelving was noticeably empty. There was not a single food item in sight. The man had consumed everything down to the empty sugar containers, ketchup bottles, and salt and pepper shakers.

There was nothing left.

"Fuck!" Ford yelled, slamming a fist against the walk-in door. His sudden outburst made me flinch. He slid down to the ground with his back against the wall, his shock unmistakable.

"He starved to death," Ford said. "We came all this way for nothing."

We wrapped the man in his blankets like a mummy then carried him down the stairs to a bedroom where we placed him in a bed and shut the door. We spent the night in the lobby, carefully moving around the evidence of the man's life here. We built a roaring fire and sat in silence next to it. There was nothing left to say. Ford knew like I did our last option was to go to Ashford.

The starved man proved people had survived the virus, but it was a roll of the dice about the outcome. I considered this man's existence these last few months. He had found himself here alone at the end. Instead of leaving, he holed up like we had in Sunrise and made it his home. He developed a system to get water. When the weather turned, he stocked the interior with enough firewood to last the season. He had to know his food supply was dwindling. I wondered why he did not choose to leave when he realized it would not be enough to sustain him. How many weeks did he feed himself the smallest amounts he could, trying to make it last? Was there a point of no return? Too weak to go and not enough to last? He was a reminder about the world we lived in and what it could mean for us if we did not find a way.

The dead are heavy. I had carried enough bodies to know. His body was frail. For a person of his frame to be so insubstantial, I knew he had prayed for sustenance trapped in this mountain fortress.

In the morning, we exited the inn the same way we came in. We pulled on our micro-spikes and made our way out into the crystal-line morning. We did our best to navigate without a road or trail to guide us.

Winds were high at the peak of Rainier, the snow blowing off the top formed a lenticular cloud like a spaceship in orbit. We decided to check the Visitor Center knowing we might only find gifts of huckle-berry flavored popcorn or chocolate. At this point, it was all calories. A door had been left open, and the snow had blown inside, creating a natural slide into the building. We went in.

The Paradise Visitor Center was an open floor plan with high ceilings and long walkways overlooking the first floor. It was a newer building evidenced by the metal girders bracing the rafters and sup-porting the walkways. I made a direct line to the gift shop and found what I expected.

The shop was frozen in time, preserved exactly as it would exist on any day. The shirts hung from the wall, displayed with care. Mugs, postcards, and coasters were all lined up and arranged in neat stacks on tables and racks. Unwashed, damp, and smelling of woodsmoke, I felt out of place standing in the middle of the pristine room. Ford had not come in behind me. The candy and food items were gone. It was hard to admit defeat, and I sensed he would be too frustrated to see it for himself. I stood for another moment taking in the way the shop appeared and feeling like a time traveler visiting another when. I returned to the lobby and was surprised to find Ford beaming.

"Look at these!" he said. He held up a pair of snowshoes and a set of trekking poles. "These will help us get around. I hope I got the right size for you."

Ford insisted on checking the employee housing near the south parking lot. The snowshoes were better than the microspikes for the depth of snow we found ourselves in, but they took getting used to. It was like strapping giant flippers to the bottoms of my feet and walking through mud. I practiced lifting my knees high and setting my hips apart to avoid dragging or tangling them. It required finding a whole different rhythm than what I was used to. I kept falling out of sync and stepping on my own shoes. Ford, of course, found his cadence with ease and pushed ahead of me.

The employee housing was like a giant resort home with an enviable mountain view, one that was nonexistent this morning. The cloud front from the day prior had moved in overnight, and it was presently threatening to drop snow. There was no more discretion about breaking a window, and Ford did not hesitate to do exactly that.

While elated by finding the snowshoes, his disappointment was plain. I could see it all over him. It was rare for him to carry anger like this. He was quiet, reticent, to the point he felt cut off from me, and I was unsure how to interact with him.

The glass fractured and shattered on the second hit, tinkling as it broke. The venture into the house was short lived. There was nothing in the kitchen. It was obvious someone had been here, likely the starved man in the inn.

In one of the bedroom closets, Ford found a box with a few freeze-dried meals. Somehow, it had been overlooked. The meals were loaded with calories. It was a good find, but it was not enough. The snowshoes and meals were barely worth the effort to get here. We returned to Longmire defeated.

It is commonly known that bad luck comes in threes.
This was no different in the world after the virus. When we returned to Longmire, despite the darkening sky, Ford went to check our trap lines. I suspected he wanted a moment alone. I went inside and lit a fire in the hearth before peeling off my outer layers.

Ford came in jubilant, holding up two small rabbits.

"Rabbit stew tonight," he said. After removing his snowshoes, he went through the dining room into the kitchen. I heard him call my name. I was satisfied the fire would catch, so I followed him.

"What's up?" I said as I entered the dining room. He held the rabbits in one gloved hand but was surveying the mess of chewed up boxes and bags on the ground, food scattered everywhere. I scanned the mess. A box of macaroni was strewn across the dining room floor. Boxes and bags had holes gnawed in them. A rodent had quite a feast on our stores.

"Mice," Ford said, "and more than one. Got a spare housecat lying around?" I rubbed my face with both hands. Ford walked into the kitchen and set the rabbits on one of the counters.

"Glad I got these. I reset the snares. Hopefully, we will have more tomorrow," he said, returning to the dining room. I stood there, helpless.

"We clean it up, Peri. We find a better place to store our food where the mice can't get it," Ford said.

"We have to go to Ashford. We have no other choice. I'll go alone if I have to," I told him, matter of fact. He did not respond. Instead, he went back into the kitchen to break down the rabbits. It made me angry, Ford's inability to accept my judgment call. Something had to be done. Later, he suggested I come watch him skin and clean the hares. I chose to busy myself with the fire instead, ignoring him as he had done to me. As the stew simmered away, he strung paracord across the dining room.

"We need to hang the food," he said. I sighed, frustrated, and went to collect pillowcases to bag everything up. The mice had gotten into so many items, I wondered how much time we had lost to their theft.

The next blow came a few days later. Ford and I went out to check our snare lines. At our first trap, we found red snow and tufts of matted fur. Something had stolen our rabbit out of the trap.

"Fox," Ford said simply, his head down as he cut the snare from the tree. "They are notorious scavengers. Not like we made it hard. A snared rabbit is easy prey. There's no point in resetting it, the fox will be back now that he found dinner here." The next snare had nothing. But the third was another bloody mess, all that was left behind was a rabbit's foot. Ford picked it up, the bloody joint still attached. He ran his fingers over the soft fur. My stomach turned.

"That dream. Paradise. Mice eating our food. Now this. Did you know a white deer is usually a good omen? But when I dreamt about her, when I saw the blood running from her eyes, I knew it wasn't. See this? A rabbit's foot. It's supposed to be lucky, but this isn't lucky," Ford said. He shook his head, demoralized, and worried.

We checked the rest of the traps. The pull snares remained set having caught nothing. I added some brush around them. A third snare we found blood and nothing else. It was uncanny how fast the fox had found our trap line and hunted it. In the thick of winter, we were not the only ones hungry. Ford stood over the blood splatters in the snow. He sighed in a deep and resigned way.

"You're right, Ashford it is," Ford said, looking up at me. He shrugged and shook his head, but behind his eyes, there was unmis-takable fear.

We made the trip to Ashford a week later after another bout of heavy snow. On the first day it relented, we set out. We strapped on our snowshoes to make the journey. We did not know the next chance we might have to make the trek. It was a dreadful day by weather standards with intermittent snowflakes and icy gusts of wind driving against us. The mountain and surrounding foothills were socked in by the cloud cover and low hanging mists. Snow was falling at higher elevations.

Ford had outfitted the wagon with a pair of antique skis procured from the inn's dining room wall and attached to our cart using strategically placed zip ties. We packed our camping gear as a precaution, not knowing where we might be spending the night. There was no way to be sure if it was safe to stay in any of the buildings near Ashford or if we could even enter the town. The distance from Longmire was twelve miles, which was a moderate day of travel by foot. The road was fortunately flat. We left before the sun rose expecting to arrive long before nightfall so we could find a safe place to take shelter.

We ventured towards the entrance of the park. Ancient redwood trees soared into the sky. The groves along the road held some of the largest trees I had ever seen. At points, the road was paved around them. Their rich red-brown bark was covered in small mint green lichen. Fairy balconies clung to their surface despite the frigid cold. Snow accumulated on those perches.

We trekked on, slow at first, but gaining speed once we each found our rhythm. We arrived at the archway announcing entry to Mount Rainier National Park, and I stopped to look up at the sign bedecked in snow. In a life past, people parked here to take pictures and memorialize their visit. In the present, the road was empty and covered under a downy white layer. I missed Su-Jin so much in that moment my heart physically ached.

We hiked in silence, each taking turns pulling the newly fashioned sled. The skis made the wagon move with ease. It was in marked contrast to the difficulty we had on the trail to Longmire. Between the weight of the wagon, our heavy gear, and learning to move with the additional weight of snowshoes, I disappeared into myself. The exertion became a meditation; somewhere between the warmup and exhaustion, I found peace envisioning the future that existed after us.

I imagined the road beneath our feet washing away, devoured by the flooding rivers, and erasing the evidence of our progress. Trails growing over, disappearing into distant memory until the wild spaces no longer knew the foot of man. Alpine regions healing, sloughing off the civilization that had destroyed them. Buildings collapsing under the weight of moss and mushrooms, consumed by the earth. The erupting volcano sending plumes of smoke into the stratosphere, and violent mudflows pouring into the glacial riverbeds spanning the state. I dreamed these places open, untamed, and free. In my mind the face of the Earth wiped clean of humanity's imprint.

We reached the Nisqually entrance before noon, breaking my reverie. After this point we would reenter what was left of civilization, leaving the park boundary behind. Outside the entrance, we could see the motels and lodges that littered the highway. We stopped to eat our lunch, propping ourselves up against an entrance booth to split a freeze-dried packet cooked on our stove. The cars used to line up here for miles. The meal, something with noodles, a red sauce, and odd little balls of meat, was hot and delicious, and when it was gone, I wished there was more.

"What if we stop and see if these motels have anything? Or go another six miles?" Ford asked. I considered this, weighing the options. I knew Ford had his fears about what we might find in Ashford, but I was hopeful.

"We keep going. If we are desperate, we know these are here. We won't have time to check both today. They will be here later in the season too," I said.

Between swaths of cottonwood forest and blackberry brambles, there was a scattering of buildings, mostly lodging for tourists but some homes. The buildings came more frequently as we closed the distance. All the structures were dark. Cars were parked outside, but if there were bodies, they were hidden under the snow. It was a relief they were unseen. I had seen enough corpses to last a lifetime.

I looked over at one point, and Ford was carrying the gun in the open as we walked down the middle of the highway. I hoped it would deter anyone we might encounter.

A field opened up beside us where a herd of elk were grazing. A haze hung over them, the collective steam from their hot breath shooting out from their nostrils. They pawed at the ground to reach the grass underneath. We watched them for a time.

Past the field was an old Victorian-style house remodeled into a café. To see it there alone made me somber, and I wondered how long it would remain. I could see the cluster of buildings ahead where the grocery was. Snow fell in large, fat flakes, swirling all around us. The only sound was the crunch of our snowshoes and the sled gliding along. Ford fell into step beside me. His eyes shifted to the building fronts and balconies of motels.

"I don't think anyone is here," I told him. I was ready to call it a day. My legs were tired, and the cold was beginning to seep under my outer layers. As we neared the store, I felt, rather than saw, Ford tense at my side.

"Peri," he said, his tone alarmed. I looked up. In front of us, nearly a city block away, stood a small woman aiming a shotgun at us.

"You can both turn around and go back the way you came!" she yelled. The sound echoed off the empty buildings. Ford held up the handgun by the butt, pinching it between thumb and forefinger, and slowly set it down in the wagon. He put his hands up. I did the same.

"We need food!" I called. "Is there anything left in the grocery store?" Her hold on the gun faltered a little, then she adjusted and pointed it at me. My heart dropped into my stomach.

"Why should I help you?" she said. She was young, I could hear it in her voice. It was the voice of a child.

"I'm Ford, this is Peri. We came from Longmire. We have been staying there since the virus came. We are running out of food and won't survive the winter. We only came for food," Ford called. The girl was silent in response.

"How do I know you won't shoot me?" she finally replied.

"We only have the handgun, there's a hatchet in my pack," I responded. "It's all we have. We only came for food."

"I am going to take off my pack, Peri will do the same. We'll put them in the wagon and take a walk so you can check for yourself. If you want to take it and leave us with nothing or shoot us, you'll have the chance," Ford told her.

"Ford," I hissed.

"If we want her to trust us, it's the only way," he snapped back.

"Your coats too!" she yelled.

Ford unclipped his buckles and placed the pack in the wagon, followed by his coat. Once he had backed up about twenty feet, I did the same begrudgingly removing my jacket.

The girl lowered the shotgun and approached. She did not hesitate.

"Back up!" she yelled. We did as ordered. It was freezing without the extra insulation. She pulled the handgun out first, checked the ammunition, and emptied the bullets into her palm. She slid the ammo into her pocket and the gun into her waistband. She was hardly dressed for the weather. Her hands were bare, she wore a heavy sweatshirt and a knit hat over jeans and a pair of snow boots. She had chestnut hair cut short and a small, upturned nose.

I waited, tense. She was going to take everything and kill us. Ford looked on, his face unreadable.

"Look," she said, as she opened and sifted through our backpacks. "I won't hesitate. If either of you try anything, I will shoot you. And it might not kill you, but I guarantee you will regret it after you are picking buckshot out of your face. There's food in the store. You, bring the wagon. Both of you in front of me."

She pointed at Ford. The girl took several steps back, pointed her firearm and waited. Ford took a few cautious steps forward, grabbed the handle of the wagon and turned his back to her as he pulled it. I fell in step behind him, and the girl came behind me.

"What were your names?" she asked.

"Peri," I said, "and Ford."

"My name's Beth," she replied. We reached the store front, which was part of a mall of shops connected by a shared walkway and awning. Beth instructed Ford to leave the wagon under the eave so it would be out of the snow. She allowed us a moment to remove our snowshoes.

"Inside, one of you can get what you need while the other sits on the floor where I can keep an eye on you. I'm not messing around. You can get your food and leave," she told us.

The three of us filed inside. It was too dark to see except for light spilling down from a stairwell at the back of the store. Behind us, Beth switched on a lantern. Ford still wore his headlamp from our early departure. He slid it onto his head and turned it on, aiming it at the ground.

The market was small, with five aisles running the length of the store. It smelled of spice and citrus. A refrigerated section was built into the back corner, but without power, it sat empty. By the register, a small display stood full of handmade soaps and lotions. The shelves were stocked with a variety of dry goods. It was exactly what I had hoped to find. We stood there looking around at all of it when I caught Ford's eye. The tension evaporated, and we both laughed.

"I told you," I said to him. Ford plucked up a basket from the stack by the entry.

"You told him what?" Beth asked. I smiled at her despite myself then sat down on the floor as she had instructed.

"I told him there would be food here. He wanted to stop and check all the motels between here and the park entrance," I replied, touching a bag of potato chips on a display next to me. Just looking at them made me hungry.

"There's not much to find," she said, "other than a lot of dead people and their luggage."

"There was nothing useful?" I asked. Beth looked uncomfortable for a moment.

"You wouldn't find much food, and I already checked for anything I could use like medicine." She backed away, angling the shotgun downward, watching both of us wearily. The girl could not have been a day over eighteen. I noted the dark circles under her eyes. Her face had the slack look of someone who needed a good night of sleep. I was too aware of the gun pointed at my neck but knew if she intended to shoot us, she would have already. She was trying to help but had no reason to trust us.

"Thank you," I said to her. "We came a long way. We need this." Beth frowned and looked to the back of the store, lifting the shotgun again to my face. I winced at the sudden movement then heard a noise come from the direction she was looking in. There were tiny feet on the stairs, followed by the giggle of a small child. Beth looked alarmed. Her eyes darting between the door and Ford. Her vulnerability had been exposed.

"Ford, don't move!" I yelled, not taking my eyes off the gun.

"This was a bad idea," she said. "You two need to go!" My hands went up again. The floorboards below Ford's feet stopped creaking as he froze behind me. The sound of small footsteps came running down the aisle, and a little boy appeared at Beth's side.

"Beth, Beth, the baby's awake," he told her, looking up at her with giant brown eyes under a mop of dark curls.

"Ok, bud, we have company," she told him. Her voice changed when she talked to him, taking on a softer, gentler pitch. He noticed us then and hid behind Beth's leg, peering out at us from behind her.

"My name is Thomas," he said.

"Hi Thomas, my name is Peri," I said, waving at him. The boy played shy but smiled from behind Beth's leg.

"Go back up and wait for me," she instructed him, still pointing the shotgun at me.

"Okay," he said, scampering back up the stairwell. When he was gone, Beth turned back to me.

"As I said, time to go."

"You have kids here?" I asked, the words out before I could stop them.

"Are you alone?" Her face told me what I needed to know.

"Do you need help?" I pressed further. Beth shook her head then lowered the shotgun.

"Don't make me regret putting this down," Beth said, her eyes were pleading with us. We lowered our hands but did not move from our positions.

"Do you need help?" Ford asked again.

"No, thank you. Really, we are doing okay," the girl said. I could not even imagine what her experience had been for the last four months.

"We can head to the other store," I offered. She considered this.

"You are already here. Take what you need and move on," Beth said. I was not reassured but chose to take her word despite her vacillation.

"Ford, go ahead. Get enough to last us awhile. We'll figure the rest out later." I locked eyes with her. She nodded and took a couple steps back. Beth's eyes kept going to the door where we could hear the baby begin to make gentle fussing sounds.

"Do you need to get the baby?" Ford asked. "We can go outside and wait. We aren't here to hurt anyone. We only came because we had no other choice."

"No, she'll be fine a few more minutes. You said you were from Longmire?"

"Yes," I replied. Ford hesitated then returned to selecting items off the shelf.

"Have you been there the whole time?" she asked.

"No, we were both hiking the Wonderland trail when everything fell apart. We stayed in Sunrise until the end of summer then moved to Longmire for the winter," I replied.

"You both hiked the Wonderland?" Beth asked, a hint of surprise in her voice. "I grew up here, lived here my whole life. My friends and I spent a lot of time in the park."

"I grew up north of here in a town like this one, with the mountain in my backyard," I told her. "Did you stay here through the virus?"

She looked crestfallen, glancing over at the stairwell again. Before she could answer the patter of feet returned, and Thomas appeared in the aisle in front of me.

"Wanna see my book?" he asked. I was caught off guard. I looked to Beth, but Thomas did not wait for a response and sat in my lap, opening the picture book. His warm weight in my lap made me relax, and I could smell the baby shampoo in his curls. It reminded me of something innate to my nature. Something protective. He pointed to the pictures, excitedly telling me the story. I looked to Beth again who had pointed the weapon away and was watching, waiting to see what I would do next.

"You see how the mouse cuts his hair?" Thomas giggled. "He made a big mess!" I could not help but smile.

"What happens next?" I asked him.

"He can't read yet. We are working on it," Beth said. Something in her shifted, she eased when she saw me connect with the boy. Why she chose to trust us I could not guess. I knew a different person might have used the child for leverage.

"You two are the first grownups I have seen since it happened," Beth said." I thought someone else would come. We saw it on the news, the president telling everyone to stay home. My dad went out to get something. He told me not to go anywhere, said he'd be right back. He never came home. I waited five days. I was too scared to leave. Cell phones stopped working on day three. After five, the power went out. I took his old pickup and drove over to a friend's place to see if they were there. When I went into their house, they were all dead. I thought the military was supposed to come. They never showed up. No one did." She paused, lost in thought, and continued, "They aren't mine, and they aren't my brother and sister. I found them, and they were the only two left."

"I looked for others when I saw the town. I hoped to find anyone still alive. I found Thomas wandering down the middle of the street. I took him home and fed him. He told me his parents were asleep, but he couldn't remember where he lived. The next day, Thomas and I came back into town to see if anyone else made it. Maybe I'd find his parents. We were driving around when he heard Charlie. I went in and got her out of that house. She'd been in her crib— I don't even know how long. I think when her parents got sick, they left a bunch of bottles in her crib, but they were all empty when I showed up. She was starving. Took five days for the diaper rash to heal. Poor thing. It's been the three of us since."

"Wow," I said, "you and two kids since August?" I tried to imagine this young woman, little more than a child herself, undertaking such a task, and it left me awestruck.

"Who else was going to take care of them?" she said, shrugging.

Ford set the overloaded basket next to the door and reached for another. Beth looked on in silence. I do not know what made her change her mind.

"Why don't you both come up? I need to get Charlie," she said. Thomas stood and trailed behind Beth. I stood up, glancing over at Ford confused, and then followed her up the stairs.

The space above the store was an apartment with a single room and a bathroom off the back of the main living area. I immediately understood why she had chosen this location aside from the access to a food supply. Big picture windows lined each wall, and you could see the road in either direction for miles.

A wood stove sat in a corner with fencing around it. I could feel the dry heat it put out and smell whatever was cooking in the cast iron pot on top of it. Occupying the center of the space was an orange-brown sofa and a lime-green armchair straight out of the seventies. The linoleum in the kitchenette was cracked and peeling. In the center of the room, children's toys and books were scattered. Fake wood paneling lined the remaining walls. This space was warm and lived in. It felt like home here, the room reminding me of the old house I grew up in.

Beth disappeared into the bedroom and returned with a red-faced toddler with a headful of blond hair. She was sniffling but settled into Beth's arm, resting her head on the older girl's shoulder and taking deep shuddering sighs.

"This is Charlie, short for Charlotte. She is about a year and a half, give or take," Beth told us. "I think she has an ear infection."

"Hi Charlie," Ford said, waving at her. She watched him, giving no response.

"You guys can sleep on the floor in here tonight. I need antibiotics for her, and I can't seem to find any," she said. "I think a trade is fair. If you help me find medicine for her, you can have all the food you can carry and then some."

Things have an odd way of lining up. Being in the right place at the right time. Or the wrong one. When people feel familiar, and you have no idea why. Signs and symbols; how when you see them, they are everywhere like glaring beacons from the universe. I thought of the RV, the one with the family, and how nothing made sense to me as I stood in that space, except the saltines inexplicably linking the past to the present like a thread. Now, standing here in a stranger's living room, another thread linking the antibiotics I found there to the bottle in my backpack downstairs. Right place, right time.

"We have amoxicillin." I replied. "I will have to check if they are expired, but I don't think they are. They are capsules too. You can mix the powder in her food. They are yours." Her eyes grew wide, relief washed over her.

"Are you kidding?" Beth smiled, daring to be hopeful. She looked between us to be assured we were serious. "She hasn't slept much in days. I could hardly step away to look for medicine. Are you sure?"

Ford and I nodded in unison.

"We're sure," I replied. "You had no reason to let us in, no reason to help us. It's honestly the least we can do. Because of you, we are going to make it through the winter."

"Thank you. There's some soup on the stove if you two are hungry. Thank you so much," Beth replied then spoke to Charlie. "Did you hear that, baby girl? You'll be right as rain in no time!"

She indicated to a pot of something on the wood stove that was filling the room with its wonderful aroma. Beth gathered some bowls and spoons with the baby on her hip then handed them to us.

"Go ahead," she offered. After we had dished up and were helping ourselves to a rich soup of chicken, pasta, and mixed vegetables, we spoke some more. The tension was gone, and the children were playing happily on the floor between us.

"Where are you guys headed next?" she asked, settling in herself with a bowl of soup. She was self-possessed in a way I could never imagine being at her age.

"Back to Longmire," Ford replied, blowing on a steaming spoonful.

"Why stay in the park?" she asked.

"Safer. Away from people," I replied, feeling sheepish talking to a young woman who was managing with two kids under the age of five.

"We wanted to stay in the park. Next summer we plan on hiking the trail once more then heading south," Ford said. Beth nodded.

"What about you?" I asked. She frowned and considered the question.

"I don't honestly know. We've been fine so far." She threw a look at the children. "There's houses up in the hills, I am thinking of moving into one of those. There's one I have been checking out. It's like a sanctuary. The people who lived there were homesteaders. We would have everything we need. It's inevitable someone else will come. We've been lucky—" she trailed off.

"You can come with us," Ford offered. It was a weak suggestion but not because he did not mean it. Beth appeared to be better off here than she would be with us in the park. She shook her head.

"Thank you, but I think this is the best place for the three of us," Beth said.

The next morning, we strapped into our snowshoes, loaded up as much food as we could carry, and said our goodbyes. Beth told us to come back when we needed to restock. She assured us we were always welcome. We got a half mile down the road when I reared on Ford.

"Should we have offered to stay?" I asked. Ford shook his head.

"She's strong enough to handle herself," Ford replied.

"It feels wrong, she's just a kid," I insisted, stopping in the road to face him. The feeling had been nagging since we left. I wanted to go back. We could help her take care of the kids. We could help take care of her.

"Did you see her scars?"

"Scars?"

"The ones on the back of her neck? The ones on her arms? The cigarette burns. They were still pink like they only just healed," he replied and walked around me. "She didn't ask us to stay. This is probably the safest she's ever been. No adults to tell her what to do. No one putting hands on her. She clearly knows what she's doing. I bet she was taking care of someone before this. Probably the same someone who put those burns on her."

I realized for Beth the virus was a gift.

We returned to Ashford once a month through the winter, staying with Beth and visiting with the children when we did. The visits felt like returning to family. We ate together, talking and laughing about life before the virus. Each time I wanted to ask her to let us stay, and each time I suppressed the urge, recognizing Beth never made the offer. She gave no indication whatsoever she needed help or wanted it. Not even a hint.

When we returned in March, we found the small apartment cold and dark. I was afraid something had happened to them, but when we scoured the room above the store, we found the children's clothes and toys were gone. On the fridge, in colorful magnetic letters were the words:

WE R OK

Below was a crayon drawing of a heart signed by Thomas. I stared at the statement, trying to determine if I believed her. Folding the drawing and placing it in my pocket, I decided I did. Beth deserved her sanctuary.

I want to show you something. For a moment, let me bring you along. Find a quiet place, embrace a moment of solitude. Sit. Take a deep breath. Now come with me.

Witness the first signs of spring. The snow melts, slow at first, and then all at once. The ice releases its stranglehold. Feel the sun warm the earth. The foliage reappears from dormancy below the snow, pale in color and scrawny. Under the rays of the sun, the plants are restored. New growth emerges in every shade of green, the palette of Mother Earth, from vibrant chartreuse to dusky pine.

Flowers bloom, the most resilient first: Pacific Trillium and beargrass, followed by red Indian paintbrushes and white avalanche lilies. They cover the meadows and worship the sun, each with its own special color and shape. Each with a pretty name: high mountain cinquefoil, Alpine aster, tiny Bellflower, Columbian lewisia, queen's cup, western moss heather, Lewis' monkeyflower. Flora found nowhere else, unique to this place, and with such a short life. Some blossoms so rare and exquisite a person could walk every corner of the park and never find them. They are a gift of life after the desolation of winter.

Watch the animals return. Two kits play in the meadows of Berkley Park, each a light orange, the color of a late summer sunset, with black dipped ears and tails. They harass a small lavender butterfly as it visits the wildflowers that grow here. The young foxes are rough and tumble, like small children, growling and nipping at each other. They play together against the backdrop of a snowy white volcano. The days are warm again, but every morning, the earth is dew kissed and smells of clean alpine air.

See the black bear amongst the huckleberries in a dense redwood grove. The scent of the berries faint and sweet while the bear snuffles through the shrubs sucking the ripe purple fruit off their branches. He lazily rolls onto his back and bends a branch to his mouth. He is young and winter scrawny but putting on weight. His coat looks soft and full. He regards his surroundings without interest, claiming this patch as his own.

Feel the cold spray of the thundering waterfall. Silver Falls is a torrent, full of snowmelt and fresh rainwater. It powers over cascading landings, falling the final forty feet into the plunge pool below. The basin is a swirling cloud of mist thrown by the Ohanapacosh River, a dancer encircling the spray around her like a scarf and throwing it high in the air. The narrow canyon downriver channels the water away, churning tiny bubbles like champagne. At times, the color of the water is crystalline blue like a gemstone and others aquamarine, appearing lit from below like a mermaid's cove.

Smell the faint, fetid scent of mud-filled hot springs. No more than puddles of lukewarm mineral water but revered in their time. It had been a sacred place. The land was stolen, like many others before it was drawn into the park boundary and guarded against private interest. Ironically appropriated to be a place of healing, the curse of that theft followed those who attempted to harness and profit from it. Misery and illness prevailed, but not before the thriving enterprise turned the hot springs into mudholes. Man's alterations to the environment, man's presence, had destroyed the resource like so many glory seekers who came before.

Visit the burned landscape of Grand Park and the charred remains of the surrounding forests. Listen to the trees crackle and break in the summer winds. It is a haunted place. The blackened charcoal touches the fallen and standing logs alike. But there is hope here. Some of the trees survived, still evergreen to clash against their stripped, soot-covered brethren. Swaths of meadow remain unburned, and the wildflowers return here too. Fireweed and purple broadleaf lupine are prevailing along the forest floor, reminding the land of what it once was. A reminder that life rises from the ashes.

See the majesty of the mountain. Do you know her true name? Ask for the wisdom of the trees who whisper it in the wind. Tahoma holds many secrets. Can you find the elk head she hides in her northern face? Or the Chinook salmon carved into her glaciers? She is surrounded by her sisters, each a beauty in their own right. Once, they shot fire into the sky and reshaped the world. A sight to behold in a different time. Tahoma will rage again. Her glaciers will shatter and melt, her ridgelines will fracture and fall. She will don a new face as captivating as her last. A constant companion on this journey; you will see her many faces and know her many names. She is glory. She is grandeur. She is mighty. She is magnificence.

Feel the trail below your feet. The earth and stone. Smell the air. Cool and clean. Breathe. Can you see it? Can you see? See.

Summer arrived, and the park was ours to explore. A stunning place I never wanted to leave; this experience, the majesty of the mountain, the life that grew here. I absorbed everything I could and held it close to my heart with the knowledge our time here was ending. We spent our days on the trail moving, as fast or as slow as our bodies required. We swam in icy alpine lakes, we wore crowns made of wildflowers, we howled at the moon and danced beside nighttime fires. There was no better place to be at the end of the world.

Through it all, we knew the reality that existed eight months after the pandemic had wiped the slate clean. Access to resources in the cities and towns would be growing scarce, people would push the limits of their boundaries, and survivors would grow more desperate. I often reflected on a parable Ford once told me about the zookeeper's son.

Walking through the zoo one morning, as they fed the animals, a young man asked his father what animal in the zoo was the most dangerous. The zookeeper replied, "People often assume it is the lion or the wolf. Surprising to most is how dangerous the hippo can be, but if they guessed those animals, they would all be wrong." The young man asked his father, "So if it isn't the wolf, or the lion or the hippo, which animal is the most dangerous?" The zookeeper turned and looked at his son then replied simply, "Man."

We completed our first hike around Rainier and after much discussion, agreed on a second before moving on. Ford deserved to finish his thirtieth Wonderland circuit, which sounded like an appropriate accomplishment to reach before leaving the park for good. We were being sentimental, which was our first mistake. Attachment was for the old world. Our second mistake was stopping in Mowich.

The campground was a different place with the presence of the sun, but it still left me feeling unnerved. Fragments of the shredded yellow tent were scattered across the camp sites, the brightly colored material muted with grime. The bones were gone, but I suggested we set up on a flat spot by the lake anyway. The main camp felt like a cemetery, the memory of the man in the tent fresh in my mind.

The first night we skipped stones across the water until it was too dark to see how far they glided along the lake. Our camp was tucked away in the trees as far from the main area as we could get. The following day, we hiked to Tolmie Peak.

The Tolmie Peak Fire Lookout was a popular tourist spot, the destination showcasing the mountain and its surrounding foothills from an incredible vantage point. Before the virus, people from all over would brave driving miles of potholed gravel road to reach the trailhead. It was a well-known and much-loved hike, second only to the Fremont Lookout. We hit the trail, the sole travelers on the path.

When we reached Eunice Lake, we stopped to admire the lookout from below. Encircling the turquoise water were thousands of avalanche lilies in shades of snow-white, pink, and lavender, rocking back and forth in the airy breeze. It was already warm, and I was questioning the decision to hike later in the day instead of early morning to avoid the heat.

"Did you know there was a double suicide at the lookout?" I asked Ford, swatting away the mosquitos floating around my head.

"That's dark, Peri, but not altogether surprising. Mount Rainier sees its share of death," he replied, shading his eyes from the sun as he gazed up at the structure.

"It was quite a mystery. They weren't local, and the road wasn't open at the time, so they would have had to hike the nine miles from the gate. That would have been a massive undertaking on its own except they never found a vehicle. There were rumors their clothes were completely out of touch with the season. They had no packs, no coats. There was a handwritten letter, on a scrap of paper with a quote about the apocalypse, which seems ironic now," I told him as we departed from the lake.

"A pact?" Ford asked.

"That's how it seemed, but so much of it didn't track. I still think about it. No one ever resolved what happened, but something about it doesn't sit right with me. A few years back there was a hiker on the trail doing the Mother Mountain Loop. He left from Mowich. They thought one of the bridges over the Carbon was out, and he tried to cross rather than turn back. They never found him. They searched until the weather forced them to stop. It was heartbreaking," I said.

"I remember hearing about that."

"Or the other guy, who walked out of a mental hospital, and stole a car. They found the car here. Not a single soul saw him, he left absolutely no trace behind except a year later, they found his shirt hanging off a tree on the trail without a spot on it. Even last year, an older gentleman came, about your age, and was camping outside the park.

Dropped dead of a heart attack, but the autopsy showed no trace of heart disease. I heard the medical examiner couldn't even confirm it was his heart, they just couldn't figure out what else happened. The family said he didn't smoke or drink, ate right, and exercised."

"Sometimes people pass, no rhyme or reason," Ford said.

"It's strange, events cluster here. Every time something happens, it's always in this area," I replied as we climbed the final slope to the lookout. Rainier was on our right, prominent and regal.

We spent the afternoon at the lookout, relaxing in the sun and enjoying a modest lunch on the balcony. The view was arguably one of the best in the park. It was not as close to Rainier as Sunrise or Paradise, but it offered a panorama from this perspective like no other. Eunice Lake sat in the valley below surrounded by forested mountains, and the entirety of Tahoma's glaciated spread was before us on the horizon. It was a short side trip on our big adventure. We returned to our campsite hidden near the lakeside, following the trail circling the water's edge. I continued our previous conversation.

"Every time we come here it gives me the willies. There's something about Mowich. Like the river. I forgot about the river!" I said, excited to bolster my argument with more evidence. "I wasn't the first to go into the South Mowich, and most people who do, don't make it out. Be honest, all the warnings from other hikers are about the Mowich crossings. Why do you think that is? You have to know something about the history. Is it some kind of ancient burial ground?"

"It could be, and we wouldn't know. It was named Crater Lake originally, but they changed it to avoid confusion with the one in Oregon. They used a Chinook word: Mowich. It means deer," Ford replied.

"Are you kid—,"

Before I could finish my response, a man stepped out from the shadows of a tree. I gasped, too startled to hang on to the strange concurrence.

"Boy, am I glad to see you two! Wasn't expecting anyone to be out here," he said. He held a single hand upright in greeting. Ford froze. I watched him process for only a second then glance back to ensure I was behind him.

"Sorry to come up on you folks like this. My name is Sam," the man introduced himself. "I was hoping I could find somewhere safe." He had a country drawl, faint, vaguely Southern and at the same time, not. My immediate perception was that he had adopted the affect as an 'everyman' way of speaking, and it was meant to make himself seem simple.

He wants us to think he's safe I thought.

I gauged him younger than me by a few years. He wore a pair of dirty Carhartt work pants and a flannel with a worn vest over it. His dark hair was shorn close. A thick dark mustache covered his upper lip and stubble across his jaw. Sam turned to look across the water, and I saw the rifle slung across his back. He gave a broad, toothy smile as he met my eye. It made the hair on the back of my neck stand on end.

Sam blocked the trail to our camp. I suspected he knew where our tents were and had gone through our gear. The fact that he had chosen this spot to intercept us meant there was a chance he had watched us depart. He tried to make it look casual, appearing out of nowhere. The man was deliberate in his friendliness; he was trying too hard.

Ford gauged the situation.

"We didn't realize anyone else was out here. Haven't seen another living person in a year. Are you alright? Are you in danger?" Ford asked. Sam nodded and took a couple of steps forward.

"I came up here to hunt. I've been staying down the road. Came from Wilkeson, but things got rough with some of the people down there," Sam said.

"People?" I asked, surprised. Sam nodded again.

"There's a settlement there, but I left. Things were turning," he said, grimacing and scuffing his feet on the gravel path. My stomach dropped.

People? I thought.

"Alright. We want to hear about that. My name's Ford, this is Peri," he gestured over to me, locking eyes with me for a flash of a second. His face conveyed his concern, a momentary expression.

"Hello," I said, waving a hand. A horse snuffled from behind a tree stand, the sound startling me. I caught a glimpse of its chestnut color through the branches.

"Nice to meet you!" The man gave another aw-shucks kind of smile.

"Well, Sam, you will have to excuse us. We are both pretty hungry and ready to put our feet up," Ford said. He walked up on the man, but Sam did not give any ground. I watched as he sized Ford up, a micro-aggression. There was something wrong with his eyes. Ford gestured toward me. He was claiming responsibility for me, to let Sam know I belonged to him, as if I were an object. Ford did it to protect me, but I sensed it would make no difference to this man.

"Peri," he locked eyes with me, and inclined his head, indicating to come with him. The man did not move off the trail to let us pass until the last second when he rolled his shoulder back to allow us by. If Sam was bothered at all, he kept it hidden. The smile did not falter.

"Why don't you join us for dinner? We want to hear your experience," Ford said. Through his big dumb smile, I could see his eyes were cold and watchful.

"Sure," Sam said. "Happy to join you. Just gonna grab some food from my bag." He indicated back to the horse and walked in the opposite direction. We moved on to our campsite. When we got some distance from Sam, I whispered, "Is this safe?"

Ford considered for a moment and replied, "I don't know. I'm not sure we have any other choice. I would rather have eyes on him than not. And if there's a settlement, I want to hear about it. If something happened there, we need to know if we are in danger. He's smart to be wary of us." My gut told me his assumption was wrong.

"Ford, he isn't acting like we are a threat. I don't think this is a good idea," I told him. Sam was already walking up behind us.

"Got my own dinner," Sam smiled, holding up what looked to be like dried meat and a handful of small carrots. I was surprised to see a fresh vegetable. The last produce I had seen was in the early weeks at Sunrise. He saw me notice the carrots.

"Do you want one?" Sam asked, offering it to me. I could not resist, despite my misgivings, and when he handed it over, I took a bite, the carrot crunching between my teeth. He gave one to Ford.

"That's impressive," Ford said through a mouthful. "I'm sure I have something to share." Sam declined. Despite the offering and polite exchange between the two men, this interaction made me nervous. Sam's gesture felt false.

Sam showed no outward sign of going without. He had the filled-out look of a man who was not missing any meals; there was a fullness in his face and a heft at his middle. His skin was pale, which could be a carryover from the winter, or a life protected from the elements.

I knew how Ford and I appeared: gaunt faces, skin pulled tight over our cheekbones. The fat layer on our bodies had evaporated over long miles of hiking. Sun exposure had bleached my dishwater blonde to a paler shade and tanned my skin, leaving a smattering of freckles across my nose and cheeks. I was surprised to find them the last time I saw my reflection in a mirror. The freckles reminded me of Bryce. Ford's silver hair and scruffy beard remained unchanged, but his face, arms, and legs were a golden brown. Both of us could use a heavy meal. Sam, on the other hand, seemed well fed.

Ford built a fire over the prior night's ashes beside the lake and stuck a pot of water next to it to boil. I grabbed three empty cache buckets to serve as makeshift seats. Sam stood to the side watching us. I set the buckets down and sat on one while I rooted in my pack for my meal.

Sam nudged the bucket back a few times with his foot, dirt puffing up with each kick, then made a big show of stripping off the gun and leaning it against a nearby tree. He was a big man. The removal of the rifle was meant to put us at ease, but I was aware he both placed it within easy grabbing reach and blocked access to it with his body. He was acting casual in how he adjusted the bucket, but it was deliberate to place himself in the best position to react if he needed to. Sam sat down, his perch precarious. It was a small seat for a large man. I was satisfied he would not get too comfortable.

"What's your story? How did you two get up here?" Sam asked. I was no longer hungry but went about the pretense of preparing a meal anyway.

"I'll start," I said, maintaining a casual tone. "I was on the Wonderland Trail when the virus blew through. When I left Sunrise, everything was normal. Not even an inkling of a problem. When I came out nine days later, everyone was dead. I laid low and, thankfully, ran into Ford. We decided to stay in the park and keep hiking the trails cause why not, right? What else do you do at the end of the world? We had no idea what was happening out there and no easy way out, so we stayed."

"Funny. I've been up here to the lake a number of times hunting, and we never crossed paths until today," Sam said. It was a strange remark, like we might bump into each other at the grocery store. The park was three hundred and sixty-nine square miles of land. He was fishing for something specific, a detail not obvious to me.

"My story is similar." Ford cut in. "I had heard in passing about a pandemic. I thought it was a joke. I had no idea what was happening until I saw it firsthand in Longmire. It was horrifying. I didn't stop to find out more. I knew people were dying, I saw someone get killed. I met Peri in Summerland after hiking straight through. We were strangers, but we stayed together after that. It's been almost a year." The water boiled. Ford split the water between our meals.

We did not answer the question he wanted answered, so he chose to be direct.

"How did you survive?" Sam asked, leaning forward, bracing his elbows on his knees. Sam was reading us, estimating what we had and if taking it from us would benefit him. He was calculating his level of risk while making a play to lure us into a false sense of security.

"Well, we both already had backpacking gear from hiking the trail, and we sourced a lot from Sunrise and Longmire," I replied, remaining vague on details. Sam seemed surprised. "Really?"

Ford nodded. There was a long silence. A calculated one. Uncomfortable silences are often filled by idle chatter. Ford and I had grown comfortable with the quiet, so we waited while we finished our meals. I forced myself to swallow each bite despite my stomach's resistance.

He's a marauder I thought. We were in danger.

"Alright, my turn, I suppose," Sam said, he rubbed a palm over his buzz cut. "I lived down in Wilkeson. On the outskirts, in the sticks. When I heard the news about the virus, I stayed put. Had enough in my house to make it a few weeks. It moved fast. Probably spread at the store or the bar. Had to be. Only two spots everyone goes. Way I figure, someone had it when they went in, and everyone there had it when they walked out. It's a small town."

This part of the story was true. I grew up in the area. I knew the places he talked about and had visited them on occasion. His estimation about how it transmitted sounded accurate. I could tell by his tone of voice, the ease of his recall, and how his eyes glazed over when he travelled back to a memory. It was a time he remembered, a thought he got lost in.

"The grid went out. I was able to find gas and put it into my truck for awhile, but it got scarce. Now, it's too degraded to use. There were others: people. We sort of banded together. It was great at first. We pooled all our resources and sent out parties to gather supplies. Things were hard during the winter because we started running out of things. There was infighting, and people started turning on each other. Like that Survivor show? Factions cropped up, and everyone had their alliances. It got weird. I tried to stay out of it, but people got mad I wasn't taking a side. One guy decided he was going to be in charge, like he knew what was best and what we should all be doing. Then it went south."

He hesitated at this point in the story.

"He killed a woman. Said she was spreading lies and turning people against each other. Said we couldn't have people like that with us. I think she was turning people against him. Wasn't hard to see it was gonna get worse, so I left. I took my horse, he belonged to one of my neighbors before everything went down and headed up into the mountains. There were houses out there, ones no one knew to check, right before the entrance to the park. I stay in the houses sometimes when the weather gets bad, but mostly, I camp in the woods."

Sam kept looking up as he spoke, like he had to think about what to say next. I ascribed it to being a mark of a liar. No one has to think about what to say when they are telling the truth. I could hear it in his voice. Why else would he be alone? The story he had sold us was fiction, but some of it was true. Sam was dangerous.

"I came here to hunt," Sam said, locking eyes with me, an expression that changed into a sheepish look. "I was hoping to have some venison steak tonight."

"I could go for a venison steak," Ford laughed in an attempt to lighten the mood.

"I also came up here to lay low a bit," Sam said.

"Why is that?" Ford asked. Sam shifted his weight and looked uncomfortable. I thought to myself how well orchestrated this whole scene was.

"They sent people to follow me. I was out hunting about a week ago, and someone tore apart my camp. Stole my things. I took what I needed, of what was left, and headed here. I'm worried they'll keep looking," Sam said. I glanced at Ford. He was buying in to this narrative. My stomach turned. Frogs croaked in the reeds next to us, filling in the spaces between our conversation. Twilight had arrived, and the light was fading. Sam stared into the flames of the fire. A full moon had risen over the horizon, casting its cool ambient light over us.

"Are we safe here?" Ford asked.

"I wouldn't be here if I thought we weren't. Just glad I met up with you folks. What do you plan to do next?" Sam said. We were back to the heart of the conversation. It was a direct question after we had failed to provide the information he was wanting. A game of cat and mouse. Later, I would go over and over it in my mind, accepting eventually that nothing would have played out any different. It would have always gone the same way.

"We don't know," Ford replied, poking at the fire. "Probably head down to Longmire before winter kicks up again. We could make it another season." This was a miscalculation. There was no right answer that would not play into Sam's hand. He knew it was a half-truth at best or a flat out lie. We had a plan. Why would we be lollygagging around the park without one? We were living in a world where survival was key, a world with an unknown future, and Ford and I were acting like we were spending an afternoon at the beach. The wheels turned in Sam's mind. He concealed it well.

I believed he was trying to determine how he was going to deal with us: join us hoping we would lead him to better resources, a better situation, or discard us altogether and take what we had? I concluded later his decision had been made before he ever sat down with us, and I had never even considered the possibility. He was asking these questions to see if we would give him a reason to change his mind.

"I went ahead and set my tent up on one of the pads up there." He indicated the direction of the actual campground. He brushed his hands off on his pants, "I think I need to hit the hay for tonight, been a long day. I'm heading out after breakfast. How long you two staying?"

It sounded casual, but to me, it was everything but casual.

"We're heading out in the morning too," I replied, not making eye contact. I felt his eyes watching and measuring me. Another miscalculation. Information was the currency in this exchange, and we were in the red.

"Nice to meet you two. See ya'll in the morning," he said, plucking his gun up from where it rested against the tree and ambled off toward the campground. Ford and I were silent until we heard his footfalls disappear.

"We need to leave," I whispered. "We can't wait until morning."

"Peri, I think we will be okay if we wait," Ford replied. I shook my head forcefully.

"He isn't telling us the truth," I said. Ford looked concerned.

"Are you sure?" he asked.

"Yes," I replied. I was certain. I felt it in my bones. He meant us harm. The man in his story, the one doing the killing, was Sam.

"Alright." Ford processed what to do next. "We head to Ipsut when we can be sure he's asleep. Can't cross the Carbon with the horse. Even if he knows we went that way, I doubt he will follow if we get ahead of him. But I don't want him to hear us packing up."

I had an impulse to insist we abandon everything and walk away. We could make it to Sunrise and resupply our gear from the ranger's inventory that remained there. My urge to run was quieted by the logic of hanging onto our supplies. Resources being what they were, I thought I needed what I was carrying. It was all that stood between us and the wild. In hindsight, we should have left then.

Ford went into his tent first while a bit of light remained in the sky and packed his belongings, leaving the tent standing.

"We can stuff the netting and carry the poles when we go," he whispered. I saw what he meant and followed suit: stuffing my sleeping bag and pad, leaving a gap to add the tent. Ford pulled out the pistol, checked it was still loaded, and left it within reach covered by his pack. He had kept it hidden from Sam. I was grateful for the weapon and glad Ford kept it on his person when we went to Tolmie. I had ridiculed him about taking the gun on our day hikes, but if he had left it behind, I knew we would no longer have it.

The white face of the moon crossed the open sky and reflected on the lake beside us. It was a bright night. I was glad for this one small saving grace. We could manage to pack and leave without the aid of our headlamps. It was a warm night, even in the mountains, but my uneasiness gave me goosebumps.

We each crawled into our tents, pretending to sleep in case Sam chose to spy on us. I lay propped up by my pack, staring up at the stars through the mesh mosquito netting. A long time passed, I waited and listened to the fire die down. The moon rose over the horizon of my tent and moved across its window.

I thought about what was to come: the Pacific Crest Trail. I was both excited and afraid. What felt like a lifetime ago, I had studied the map and read about the locations. There were so many new things to see. South of our present location, and the first I could check off the list, would be Goat Rocks Wilderness. We would cross the famous Bridge of the Gods over the Columbia River. Ford said he could not wait to see the Three Sisters Wilderness, and we planned on a detour to Crater Lake to see the deep blue of the water there. If we made it far enough south, we would visit Yosemite, the Sierra Nevada, and the legendary Mount Whitney. There would be long jaunts in the wilderness, so supplies and water would have to be carefully managed. I did not know if we were fools for choosing this, but I had faith we would survive.

I caught myself drifting toward sleep a few times before the fall, so I sat up to force myself awake. When the moon began its final descent, I could no longer wait to move. Ford was asleep, signaled by the sounds of his light snores. I unzipped my tent in slow, quiet inches and stepped out in the night air, taking steady breaths through my nose. I felt shaky and sick. I was terrified of making a sound.

The knife point jabbed into my low back where my spine and pelvic bone met the second I was upright. I almost yelled, but a quick hand slid over my mouth and gripped my chin hard. The tendons holding my jaw felt like they might snap. I felt his hot breath against my ear.

"Quiet, bitch." I froze. The knife dug in a little harder. I winced, my knees buckling from the pain.

"You try anything, I will jam this into your spine, and you'll never hike again. Walk," he said. Sam had executed his counter maneuver perfectly. While I was distracted, contemplating the stealth it would require to vanish into the night, he had crept up on us without making a sound. It was stupid to assume Sam would go to sleep. I took a step, but he corrected my direction by yanking on my jawbone so hard I thought it would rip clean off. I caught myself as I stumbled. My ears rang. He jabbed the knife in harder, and a hot trickle of blood rolled down the center of my back. I did not dare cry out.

I made the mistake of forgetting a key thing about man. At our core, we are animals. Man has base needs. They can be muddied with complicated motives or history, but all stem from a primal place inside. I should have had the foresight to see this. It was never about our resources.

My thoughts raced, trying to remember everything I had been taught to do in these situations. How many articles and anecdotes had I seen and shared with information on how to stave off an attack? Each required the capability to fight, but I had no upper hand and nothing to leverage. It is hard to imagine at times the only possibility left is to freeze. Here I was again, a hostage to fear despite everything I knew. In the hierarchy of needs, survival is the basest.

He marched me in silence, forcing each of my legs forward with the weight and pressure of his body. This was not his first rodeo. He had used this tactic before. My heart raced. I tried to control my breathing, exhaling as slowly as I could manage.

Sam got me to the far side of the lake, a long walk from where we camped, and shoved me into the talus along the trail. I fell onto a boulder, my left wrist taking the brunt of my fall. It flared with bright white-hot pain. I let out a quick gasp, cradling the limb to me. Before I could roll onto my back, he was on me with the knife against my throat.

"Shut the fuck up, you fucking bitch," he hissed. I felt the blade against my Adam's apple. I swallowed, and the knife nicked my skin. The jagged boulders dug into my backside and shoulders. I tried to find purchase, but my feet kept sliding out, the gravel on the path scattering underfoot. He unslung the rifle across his back and set it outside of my reach. He was fumbling to undo his pants and take them down with only one hand. I was afraid he would slip and slit my throat open. I stayed still, the heat of him forced against me. Sam moved to take down my shorts and snorted derisively as I flinched away on instinct.

"Stupid cunt, don't fuck with me. I will cut you from neck to navel like the last bitch that tried to fight." He ripped my shorts down.

The knife pressed harder into my throat. I forced my head back against the jagged stone trying to make space between myself and its fine edge. The sharp point of a rock was grinding into the back of my skull, making my head ache.

"I knew it." I choked out. "I knew it was a bullshit story." He chuckled, fumbling with one hand to pull my underwear off when a light blinded me.

"Get off of her!" Ford's voice came over Sam's shoulder. "Put the knife down or I'll shoot."

Sam tossed a glance over his shoulder, removed the knife from my throat, and yanked up his pants. He cast a hateful glance in my direction.

Twenty feet away, Ford stood with the headlamp glaring, the only thing visible in its light was the handgun pointed at Sam's head. Sam stood tall. I could breathe again without his full body weight on me. I grabbed for my shorts with my aching wrist and lifted myself off the rocks with the other. Ford took cautious steps forward, gaining ground. Sam turned to face him, holding the knife between his thumb and forefinger.

"You already got yours, man!" Sam laughed. "Thought I would get my chance. You can't keep the last female in a hundred-mile radius to yourself! You're too old for her anyway. Bet she keeps you up all night."

"That whole story was a lie," Ford mused. "Drop the knife, friend." He planted his feet and changed his grip on the gun. He did not want to shoot. In the hung moment, a droplet of blood trickled down the front of my neck. I did not dare move to wipe it away. Sam took a step forward, then another. Ford exposed his defensive position by taking a step back.

"And if I don't?" Sam grinned. "There's no one left except me. I made sure of it. But I didn't expect you. Your fire gave you away. Could smell it for miles." His face was lit by Ford's lamp, a mask of ridges and valleys in deep contrast. The aw-shucks persona was gone. The thing he hid, the one that watched and waited below the surface, was here.

Sam lurched forward in a bluff charge to test Ford's reaction. Ford startled instead of firing. The younger man used the opening to launch at Ford with terrifying speed, tackling him into the lake.

My heart stopped. This man was about to murder my only friend in the world. There was no one to call, no help would come. It all came down to me. I was running across that lawn again, praying to make it in time. Blood rushed in my ears, my mind raced, and I fought the urge to scream. The familiar all-consuming panic moving in. I began to count backward, struggling to suppress my rising terror when something caught the corner of my eye.

The rifle leaned against the rocks, glowing in the reflected moonlight. I picked it up, feeling its weight. A shroud of calm enveloped me, and the world slowed. Seconds trickled by like sand through an hourglass, and I was able to see everything before me like I was moving against the current of time.

Ford and Sam struggled in the water. Sam had the upper hand. The knife came up, spotlighted by Ford's headlamp, and I watched in horror as it came down. Ford made a sound like the wind had been driven out of him.

Sam brought his arm up again, water spraying out from the blade. I swung the rifle around by its barrel, letting the pain sing in my wrist, and closed the distance, wading knee-deep into the water.

The knife slammed down again. When it came back up each crimson-tinged droplet refracted the incandescent moonlight. I gripped the barrel, pulled back with both arms over my shoulder, and swung the stock of the rifle like a baseball bat as hard as I could. It connected with Sam's temple with a satisfying crack. His jaw went slack, and he fell face first into the lake.

I grabbed a fistful of Ford's shirt to pull him out of the water. He gasped as he surfaced, locking eyes with me. His headlamp had come off, its light illuminating Sam's floating body on the muddy bottom of the lake.

The pain in my wrist was temporarily forgotten standing calf-deep in the lake. Ford, soaked, leaned against me breathing hard. Tears of relief welled in my eyes, all the emotion rushing into me at once. When his breathing calmed, he walked over to a boulder on the edge of the water and sat down.

"Are you okay?" I asked him.

"Peri," Ford wheezed. He pointed a weak finger past me. I turned around. Sam was sitting up on his knees, coughing up the water he swallowed. He stood up. I fumbled with the rifle, trying to aim. It was difficult to hold the gun with my injured wrist, but I did not hesitate. When I squeezed the trigger, nothing happened.

"Bolt." Ford wheezed. "Up and back then forward and down." I grabbed the black metal of the bolt. I wrenched it up and toward me, almost dropping the gun in the process, then back into position. I adjusted my grip on the weapon and put my finger on the trigger.

Sam froze when he heard me racking the gun. He slowly lifted his arms over his head, his back still to me. He turned to face me, his eyes wide with shock, but there was a darkness underneath the look, an anger. He opened his mouth to speak, and I pulled the trigger.

The rifle slammed into my shoulder and bone deep pain ripped through me. I fell back into the water, dropping the gun, dazed. I looked up at the stars in the night sky. The same sky I had gazed at every night for the last year. The painted streak of the Milky Way was coming into full view as the moon sank below the tree line. The faint lilacs and effervescent greens swirled and danced as my mind closed in on me.

"Peri."

"Peri."

Su-Jin. Her hands clasped mine. She was looking down at me with a soft smile. My heart lifted at the sight of her. Warm energy surrounded me. It was peaceful here with her.

"He needs help. You have to help him," she told me.

"But I'm tired," I replied. She smiled again. I smiled back at her, joy filling me.

"I know, but he needs you."

"I'm glad you are here. I missed you so much," I said. Su-Jin squeezed my hand.

"Help him," she said. I had the sensation of falling. And pain. Startling, surreal pain.

"Peri."

"Peri."

I fought the voice rousing me, searching for Su-Jin. Blackness faded. My shoulder was in agony. I groaned. Feeling hands on me, I screamed and resisted. My right arm dangled, useless.

"It's me! You're safe! You're safe! He's gone," Ford said. He was leaning over me, still dripping. The sky looked the same as I lay in the water. It must have only been seconds since I had blacked out. I sat up, and my right shoulder reminded me that it had provided a stopping wall for an improperly held firearm. It hung at a strange angle. Ford helped me up. And there he was. Sam. Standing there, a few yards away, watching us.

I was in shock. Somehow, Sam had survived the blast. For a moment, I was frozen by the sight of him.

"No, no, no, no," I cried.

Ford turned. "He's dead Peri. He's dead."

Sam lumbered towards me. Water dribbled from his mouth above the ragged hole the rifle had torn through his throat. The gaping wound spewed blood. He waded through the lake, hatred in his eyes, drawing closer to me with arms upraised to strangle me. Behind him his body floated in the water. Like at Sunrise. Like Su-Jin. I backed away.

It filled me with rage, a rage so cold it overwhelmed me. I would not allow this to attach to me. I would carry no shame for killing this monster. I would not permit fear to take hold and ruin me. I stood tall to face him, wanting to both laugh and spit in his face. My heart hammered in my chest, and I stood firm, fortifying my will. He reached for me, his hand caressing my cheek, and with that touch, his visage evaporated like smoke disappearing on the wind as the last sliver of the moon slipped over the ridge.

I breathed a sigh of relief, the tension releasing from my body. Sam's body remained on the surface of the lake, the headlamp spotlighting the red pool around him. I bent to pick up the light, and turned the beam onto Ford, finding him hunched over so far he was almost lying in the water. Blood covered his entire side.

"Oh god, you're hurt," I said. He waved me off.

"I'm fine, just a cut, help me up?" he lied. I grabbed his hand with my good arm. He winced as he stood straight, placing a hand over his side. We walked back to our tents, my shoulder screaming with every step. I sat Ford down on one of the buckets then dug through my bag for the first aid kit where I kept our stash of medication. I popped four ibuprofen and an oxycodone. I gave one to Ford too. He was in trouble, but I could do nothing without the use of my arm.

"I think your shoulder's dislocated, and I'm in no shape to help you," Ford said.

"I'll figure it out," I replied, walking up toward the patrol cabin. I picked up a stick along the way.

I walked up the steps of the cabin. The first aid classes never covered this. I put the wood in my mouth, tasting dirt when I bit down, and lined up my shoulder in the door frame, guessing at how to position myself. I grasped the wall on the inside of the cabin to leverage my body against it, reassuring myself the pressure would be relieved once I got the joint back in the socket.

I gathered my nerves, readying myself. I shoved, hard, and failed. Bone grinding pain flared through me. I crumpled to the ground, my mind wiped, gasping as it throbbed through my whole chest cavity. Sweat prickled on my brow, and I crouched there enduring the shock that rolled through me.

Su-Jin's words came back into my mind. I had to get through this. There was no one else to help Ford. I stood up, wincing as I leaned against the wall with my good shoulder. I panted, praying for the pain medication to kick in. I gritted my teeth, bit hard on the stick, and again, shoved my shoulder into the wall.

It locked in, bones snapped together, and for one horrifying second, pure agony slammed into me. I gasped, but the pain relented as fast as it came. I tentatively tried my right arm and was relieved to find it worked again. It ached, but it would heal.

I passed by the empty campground on my way back to the fireside. Sam had not even set up a tent. It confirmed what I already knew. He always had a plan. I came upon Ford holding his head in one palm a troubled expression on his face. He would not look me in the eye. Before I even sat, he asked.

"Did he—" Ford hesitated. The unfinished question hung in the air.

"No. You showed up in time," I replied, seating myself on the bucket across from him.

"I misjudged how dangerous he was. You warned me. I should have listened," Ford said, wiping a tear from his eye. "I fell asleep while we were waiting. I don't know for how long, and when I woke up, I heard something. It was so quiet. When I said your name and you didn't answer, I knew he had you. And I knew it wasn't good. If it weren't for the moonlight—" He trailed off, the horror of a different outcome locked in his eyes.

"I'm so sorry, Peri."

"You have nothing to be sorry for." I took his hand and squeezed it. I smiled at him, and he smiled weakly in return. His shirt was soaked with blood.

"Ford, we have to do something. You are not fine," I said. After stoking up the fire, and throwing a few branches on, I pulled my bucket closer. I lifted his shirt to inspect the wound, and he stopped me. There was a defensive wound on his hand.

"I don't think there is much you can do, Peri," he said, looking into my eyes.

"What do you mean 'not much I can do'? I need to stitch you up."

"He got me in the stomach a couple times," Ford said.

"Well, you haven't bled out yet, so he didn't hit anything critical. I can clean them out, stitch them up," I said, standing up to grab my pack. I hesitated, not knowing whether to pick it up with the swollen wrist or the recovering shoulder. I chose the wrist, reminding myself, despite the pain, I was lucky to be alive.

"Peri, if my intestine is cut, I'll get sepsis. At the very least, the wounds will get infected. We aren't in a sterile environment," Ford said.

I considered his words. I had no medical knowledge. I had never sewed anything more than a button in my life, but Ford had no other choice except me. I would have to try. I dug through the recesses of my pack and located the hard plastic case holding the sewing kit I had never used. I laid out Ford's sleeping bag beside the fire.

"Come lie down," I said. He did as I asked, understanding I would not take no for an answer. His shirt clung to his body as I peeled it off and found the two wounds, each pulsing blood.

The knife had been sharp, I knew by the clean lines of Ford's lacerations and how it had cut my skin with a glance. It would make the wounds easier to stitch, but the knife had pierced deep, evidenced by the bruising around each opening. I rejected what he was trying to tell me, choosing to believe instead, I could save him.

I pulled a fresh shirt from my bag and tore it into strips. I rinsed his cut hand with filtered water first and slathered antibiotic ointment into it, wrapping it in the pieces of the shirt. It was a significant cut into the fleshy space between his thumb and index finger. It was the best fix possible. No amount of stitching would hold it closed. He wiggled his fingers to prove nothing vital had been severed. Next, I inspected the two punctures in his gut and wished I had a gallon of iodine.

"I'm so sorry I have to do this, but it's going to hurt like hell."

Ford wanted to leave Mowich. He insisted at dawn he felt good enough to move on. He was concerned there were others coming.

"There's no one else. He was lying," I told him. "He probably killed them all." Ford, feeling some relief from the pain pill, shook his head.

"I would feel better if we left. You were right the other day, something is wrong here. Take me to Sunrise, this place is full of ghosts."

Before we left, I went through Sam's gear. He was not carrying much, which made me believe he was not lying about a nearby camp. I secretly prayed to find a bottle of antibiotics, hoping to stave off inevitable infection. I had no such luck.

For only half a second, I regretted giving our antibiotics to Beth. Ford's words at Golden Lakes returned to me: 'Abandoning someone when they need help is inhuman'. I remembered how she had opened her home to us. We would not have survived the winter without her. She showed us humanity when the world had shown her none.

I weighed the risk of traveling alone to the nearest community to find medicine. With the horse, it was doable. I pitched it to Ford who refused my pleas.

"Too dangerous," he said. "What if he wasn't lying about that part?"

I found a handful of bullets for the rifle, so I fished the gun out of the lake. We took the horse. Helping ease Ford into the saddle took all my strength. He grimaced, favoring his side, then managed to give me one of his prize-winning smiles. I smiled back but felt something inside me fracture. My hope was fading. I asked him three more times if he was sure, and he insisted.

I got his pack strapped down in front of him so he could brace himself against it and hold the reins. The pain would be excruciating, but this was the best plan I had. I forced another pain killer on him. He made a small show of declining, and then accepted. As we headed out through Spray Park, Ford told me a tale.

"Did you know that Peter Rainier never saw the mountain he was named after? He never even set foot in America," Ford told me. "Even after it was named, people still called it Tacoma, but the settlers in Seattle didn't like the mountain being named after their rival city, so they petitioned it be changed. In fact, they bribed the US Board that handled the naming, and the rest is history." He continued to tell me about the naming of the mountain, lamenting Rainier's true name had not been restored in his lifetime, but I barely heard him. I hoped after I cleaned his wounds and stitched them as best I could, it would be enough to save him. I wanted Ford to be wrong.

We never made it to Sunrise.

Ford went silent a couple miles before Cataract Valley.
He had tried to maintain his usual candor despite the blood loss
and medication. Ford slumped over his pack in an opiate stupor as
the horse kept a slow, deliberate pace on the trail. I kept my hands
on the reins, leading, since Ford was unable to guide it himself.
I stopped at Marmot Creek to fill our water as we arrived at the
campground. When I touched Ford's arm to check on him, he lifted
his head.

"Must have been powerful stuff," he slurred. "I dozed off."

"That's okay, Ford, they're powerful to make you comfortable,
but I need you to drink some water," I said, handing him his bottle full
of clean, cold water. He took several large gulps, panted, and drank a
couple more. His eyelids were heavy. I noted blood soaking through
the shirt I had put on him this morning. I told myself there were new
shirts in Sunrise.

"That's it for us today," I said. I was exhausted. The one pain pill
I had taken before correcting my shoulder was starting to wear off.
My chest was turning ugly shades of deep purple and black. The pack
rubbing against the bruises was a constant reminder. My back had
cuts and welts from being thrown into the rocks. My wrist was so
swollen the joint was almost imperceptible. I had wrapped it with the
last shreds of the torn shirt which had done little good. Everything
hurt, and Ford was not doing well.

I pitched Ford's tent, set up his pad, and laid him down. There
was a thin film of sweat on his brow, and his eyes were glassy, sliding around beneath their lids. He muttered something I could not
understand.

I made oatmeal using some of the gas we had managed to conserve. I tried to get him to eat. He took three bites before begging
off. I insisted but could see how much effort it took to lift his head. I
forced a couple more spoonfuls on him then finished the rest myself.

After urging him to drink more water, I lifted his shirt to examine his wounds. One was sealed, despite spending the day on horseback, and although the stitches were loose, it looked clean. The other continued to seep watery blood which concerned me. I cleaned my hands and applied more antibiotic ointment knowing it would do nothing for the damage inside.

I suspected the blade had perforated Ford's gut. It meant the fluid from his digestive tract was leaking into his abdomen. The wound was hot to the touch. That meant infection, which meant sepsis. Sepsis meant death. An ugly one. I did not want to think about it. I made myself eat a protein bar and took more ibuprofen. I sat over Ford through the evening, wetting a handkerchief and placing it on his forehead. Eventually, I fell asleep on the ground next to him. I did not dream.

I woke late in the morning. I came out of a fog having forgotten where I was and experienced a momentary panic having fallen asleep next to Ford in his tent. I never cleaned up dinner, and it was fortunate my error did not attract any wildlife during the night. That was the last thing I would have been able to deal with. I could not make that mistake again.

I was stiff when I moved and ached all over. I grabbed the bottle of painkillers from my pack to take one and pulled one out for Ford. I hoped by the next day I would not need to rely on the heavy artillery to make it through the day. I would not be so lucky with Ford. I lifted his shirt to check his wounds and touched the ugly one. It oozed a yellowish fluid tinged with blood that smelled bad. He continued to sleep while I made myself a meal and cleaned up.

When he woke, he coughed a few times and groaned. I kneeled into the tent opening to hand him fresh water and the pain pill. His skin was an ashen, pasty color, and his eyes were rimmed red. He drank half the bottle, which made me feel better. It was a good sign. I filtered more water and when I returned, he was sitting up.

"Hungry?" I asked. He shook his head.

"Maybe we should stay here?" I suggested.

"Where are we?"

"Cataract Valley."

"Cataract Valley," he repeated, thoughtful. He cleared his throat a few times. "I suspect we can make it to Mystic Lake today. I am sorry I faded out like that."

"Ford, you aren't well. We should stay here and rest," I said. He shook his head.

"We can make it to Mystic Lake," he said. He was firm. Or stubborn. I sighed and packed our things. I got Ford on the horse and hoisted his pack up. It was even harder to lift him today than it was the day before. I brushed it off, attributing the difficulty to my pain and fatigue. In the back of my mind, though, as faint as a whisper, I knew his strength was waning.

I checked the straps then squatted to get my pack on. My bruised shoulder flared a warning. I loosened the strap to favor that side, knowing I would feel it in my hips later. We pressed on.

We made it to the suspension bridge over the Carbon River before reaching the glacier overlook. I contemplated waking Ford to have him cross on foot, then realized he would never make it on his own. I had no other choice. I checked all the straps, pulled the leads and stepped onto the edge of the bridge. The horse balked. I knew less than nothing about horses, so I clucked at him. The gelding pawed at the ground and swung his head a bit in protest.

"Whoa," I hushed him, walking up on the animal and rubbing a hand down the front of his nose. Ford stirred, watching through bleary eyes, and tried to sit up.

"Ford, it's fine. He will come across, I think he needs to feel safe. Hang on tight," I said. Ford opened his mouth to say something and made a strangled noise.

"What's that?" I asked him. Ford pointed at his throat. I took the water bottle out of his backpack pocket and handed it to him. He took a long drink.

"His name is Henry," Ford said, indicating to the horse. I smiled. He smiled back. I ignored the sign warning to cross one at a time and prayed the bridge would hold our combined weight. The gelding kept trying to back away.

"Did you know Indian Henry had three wives?" Ford asked. He told us about Indian Henry and how he named one of his sons after the judge who ordered him to give up his plural marriages. Ford went into detail at the retelling, the cadence of his voice calming the animal.

With a lot of coaxing, I led Henry across the bridge. We went slow, his ears pinned. The bridge moved with our weight as we bore ourselves across the span high above the earth. I was careful not to look down, but in truth, I wished we had not gone this way. I spoke to Henry in short commands, quiet and firm, when he tried to avert his gaze from anything except me.

Ford finished his story about Indian Henry's hunting grounds and his mysterious gold nuggets as we reached the other side. The effort drained him, and he grew quiet again. Both Henry and I struggled to relax as we headed into the precarious section of trail where we traced our way around the Carbon Glacier.

I had forgotten about Dick Creek until we came upon it. Over time, the water had dug a channel between large, jagged boulders and slipped through the rift it had created. The crossing was a short log with no handrail.

The distance was too far for Henry to step over, and the rocks were uneven, so he could not balance on one to step to another without breaking a leg. Downstream, the hillside fell away into the Carbon River canyon. From the right vantage, I could see the soot-covered glacier. It was too steep for a horse to navigate. I turned upstream, off trail, hoping to find a place to safely cross.

Half a mile out of the way, I found a spot. A place where the stream formed a pool. Its deepness I could not determine, so I took off my own shoes and socks and waded in. This would do.

"Ford, I need you to wake up," I said. Ford had drifted again, dozing in an opiate-induced stupor. He was slower to open his eyes this time around. The glassiness in them and the weakness; it was more than the opiates.

I double-checked all the straps and after taking my back-pack and shoes across, I waded back through the creek to collect Henry and Ford. Henry was again reluctant, but came forward willing enough, balking as his hooves sank into the mud at the bottom. I calmed him, staying close as we crossed the small channel together.

The sun was high and beating down from a cloudless sky as we climbed out of the valley, no tree cover to protect us from the heat. It sapped my energy and worsened Ford's state. For once, I wished for a cooler day. I stopped to draw water at every creek and forced it on him.

Before we reached Mystic Lake, I heard a mumbled request come from behind me. I was surprised to see him awake without my prompting. Ford waved his hand at the line of trees.

"Through here," he pointed to a small dirt path leading away. We followed it a short distance until the trees cleared to reveal a tarn in the middle of a small meadow. Reflected in it was Mount Rainier. The view was stunning. Giant boulders encircled the water. The blue at this altitude was a crisp cerulean, and the mountain stood high above the lake.

"Help me down?" Ford asked. I set down my pack and allowed him to brace himself against my good shoulder. I walked him over to the edge of the water where we sat on the rim of the pond. I pulled his shoes and socks off so he could stick his feet in the pool. I pulled off my own and felt the cold water between my toes.

"This is one of my favorite spots," he said.

I remembered a similar moment with Su-Jin, sitting on the log at Mystic Lake. I recalled how she had spoken of her son. Today could not be any more different, and yet it felt the same.

"Peri, I need you to leave me here," he said. I felt a familiar twist in my stomach.

"No," I replied without looking at him.

"I want you to take the horse and head south like we planned. Go to Sunrise, get the last of our supplies. You can use Henry to carry everything. That should get you by for a while. Follow Wonderland until Fryingpan Creek then take the road to Owyhigh Lakes. On the other end, head north onto the Eastside Trail. From there, you can get on the PCT like we talked about. Like you always wanted," he gave me the route as if we had not planned and discussed this a dozen times already. He smiled at me, a beautiful smile.

"I won't leave you, Ford," I said.

He leveled a gaze at me for a long time with the same sweet smile on his face. It took me too long, but realization set in.

"No," I said, shaking my head.

"I need you to," he said.

"No," I said flatly.

"Please."

I shook my head again and turned away from him, looking out at the lake. Tears in my eyes.

"Let's stay here a few days, and we will see how you feel," I said. "You might get better." My words unconvincing to my own ears. Ford snorted.

"Peri, I'm dying. We can stay here as long as you need, but this will kill me one way or another. I am asking you to do it. In the end, I will be sick and in pain. Please."

I stared at him. Tears spilled over.

"When?" I asked him.

"When you are ready," he replied like it was a simple thing. I did not respond, and the silence hung between us, heavy.

"What will I do without you?" I asked him. He did not answer but instead took my hand. I could feel the fever through his palm, understanding he was much sicker than I had allowed myself to realize. Through all of it, he maintained his kind spirit, his nature to hold the good of the world in his heart, and his ability to smile in the face of darkness.

Sobs came from deep within me. He stayed by my side, keeping my hand in his while my heart shattered into pieces. Once drained of my tears, I was left empty and hollow. Ford finally spoke.

"This has been an incredible journey with you, Peri. I could not have asked for a better person to have this experience with. I have looped the Wonderland dozens of times," he chuckled. "I love this mountain and I love this place. It's fitting for me to stay here while you move ahead. Not because I want to leave you, I would never leave you behind, but because you need to move forward. Another winter here will be long and difficult. You need to go where you can survive. I have faith the PCT will lead you to a community of good people. People like us."

"But you won't be there," I replied.

"You are my best friend," he squeezed my hand, a single tear slipping down his cheek. "I spent so much of my life feeling like I was on my own, even when I had people close to me. I was always alone: in my marriage, with my kids, my employees, the church. I brought together a whole community around my favorite place in the world hoping to find someone to connect with, and it only made me feel more isolated. At the end of the world, I found you, and with you, I have never been alone."

I rested my head on his shoulder, struggling to find words. It took a long time for me to accept what he was asking of me.

"You've shown me I was stronger than I ever would have believed. I know who I am because of you. I love you, Ford. If this is what you want, then okay. Okay."

Three days later, I ended my best friend's life.

I led Henry down the Owyhigh trail. It was August again, and it felt like August. The clouds from the thunderstorms the night before had passed. The moisture was absorbing into the dirt as the day warmed. I stopped along the path to enjoy a handful of rain-covered huckleberries. A year ago, I thought I would never want to see another of these berries again, but today, I enjoyed them, the tartness making my jaw ache. I fed a few handfuls to Henry.

One evening, while we camped, Ford had told me a story about Henry, the horse. It included where he was born, his life before the virus came through, and how he had come to be with us. He was careful to gloss over most of the bits including Sam, but there was a long portion about a circus. With Ford, there was always a story. I set up our tents by the water, and we spent mornings watching the animals come to drink, but he never left the tarn.

Ford stopped eating altogether on the second day. He took what minimal water he could manage without getting sick. His fever came and went, then came on hard and heavy and never left. I spent most of my time trying to keep him comfortable until he grabbed my hand on the evening of the third day and gave me a look. The look that begged for me to end it.

How do you destroy the thing you love the most?

I did it because he asked me to. I did it because I loved him more than I loved myself. I did it because I could not allow my best friend to continue to suffer. I told myself it was a mercy for him even though it spelled pain for me. And I hated myself for it.

As Henry and I walked the trail, I recalled the day Ford shared his dream with me. Standing in the snow, the warning about the white deer. He told me then something bad was coming. Ford had been right all along to be worried. The white deer in his dream was Death. He had thought she was coming for me. Thinking of how he told it with the white doe placing her head in my hand. It had sounded like a warning, but I understood now, she was offering me comfort. Death has become a close friend of mine.

I kept Henry as a pack horse because he would allow me to carry more supplies. He was a docile creature, and I was glad to have his company. Before I left Sunrise, I took a detour out to the Fremont Lookout. I collected my long-abandoned cell phone from its pro-tected place in the fridge. I charged it off the still operating solar bat-teries. I brought with me a lock of Ford's hair. My hands remained raw from stacking rocks for a grave over his body.

I went out to the lookout alone and sat for a long time staring out into the distance, admiring the mountain. I held the hair and a collection of wildflowers until I finally let go and tossed them to the wind. The breeze carried it all away, down to the land we had shared, ours and ours alone for a time.

I opened my phone to scroll through the pictures from our

early days together. Here were photos of Ford and I at the top of the Burrough's hike. Another of marmots in Summerland manhandling our packs. The beauty of Indian Bar. Ford's smile. I was surprised to find Su-Jin in some, posing in front of a waterfall. Another showcasing her with the mountain. I did not remember taking these.

I missed her. I missed them both. Buried in the album was a lone picture of Bryce, I kissed his face on the screen. Despite thinking I could cry no more, I did. I never felt more alone than in that moment.

When I returned, Henry waited for me next to the Visitor Center nibbling at what ground cover existed. I was a little surprised and grateful, half-expecting him to wander off while I was gone. He was a good horse.

I followed Ford's instructions. I found the sign for the Owyhigh Lakes and followed them to connect to the Eastside trail. Eventually, it would lead me to the Pacific Crest Trail.

Owyhigh is bordered by Governor's Ridge on one side and Tamanos Mountain on the other. Governor's Ridge is a serrated range like the edge of a knife, the rocks eroded away into sharp teeth. It was an interesting formation, one I admired when we arrived at the lakes. I sat on the ground, leaning up against a log, scanning the mountains and looking up at the sky. I watched a pair of birds bathe in the water. After dozing for a short time, I had a small snack, and then we moved on. I made it to Deer Creek Camp before nightfall. Another concurrence. The doe of Ford's dream. Mowich. Things have an odd way of lining up.

It was a warm evening, and I bathed in the creek to wash off the dust and sweat. It felt good to be clean again. It felt like starting over. I went to bed without dinner. In the morning, I double-checked the bags I had rigged for Henry. It was not pretty, but it worked.

For the first time in weeks, I was beginning to feel okay, but it would be a long time before I was going to be good again. The next day I found myself at the top of Chinook Pass overlooking Tipsoo Lake. It was like walking into Sunrise on the first day. Cars, bodies, all my senses standing on end. Except I was not alone anymore. Henry was with me, and so was Ford.

By some minor miracle, his head did not reflect the injury he had sustained like Su-Jin or Sam. I had given him a dose of painkillers crushed up to make him comfortable. It might have been enough to do the job with his failing system, but I had promised him I would be sure. He still had the wounds from the stabbing. I rationalized it was because those would have been his mortal wounds despite my intervention, but I did not understand the mechanisms behind whatever magic this was. I only felt gratitude he did not bear the wounds I had given him. He never left me, although at times, he understood I needed space. It was hard to process his death with his constant presence.

He never truly left my side. He was with me through the days of crying in my tent and the days after of being unable to do anything except sleep through my utter despair. He was with me for the unending hours I spent carrying rocks to his grave until my fingers bled. My best friend.

When I reached the PCT, I turned to look back. Mount Rainier glittered white and blue in the brilliant sun, filling the horizon. She was as beautiful today as every day I spent with her. Tahoma. Mother of Waters. Wonderland. Home.

It felt like we had spent a lifetime there and for a moment, I could not take another step. I admired the mountain and felt a deep longing to return, to scrap this wild idea of going south, and head back. When I glanced over at Ford, he was watching me and smiling. It still hurt to look at him.

"Are you ready?" he said.

And I was. I turned around, tugged at Henry's reins, and headed south with the Pacific Crest Trail beneath my feet.

The End

ACKNOWLEDGEMENTS

First, thanks to you, the reader, for picking up this book and following the story to the end. I hope you enjoyed it enough to come back for the next one. I was as accurate as possible when I could be. All the mistakes were mine, but the French fries were deliberate.

To my first readers: Bill, Carol, Gina, Corrine, Jeff A., and Remle, your feedback was invaluable, but your support was priceless. A special thank you to my new friend, Shannon, for using her trail expertise to point out where I got it wrong and helping me make it right. Jeff E., your feedback made me crazy and challenged me to be a better writer. Thank you.

My cousin, Sarah, for giving me permission to steal some of her story and inspiring me to be "wild" like her. Ron for encouraging me to use my skill set to pursue my own venture. Thank you to the Wonderland Group for fielding some of my questions and providing photographs.

My dad for being so vocally supportive and always excited about what I am working on. I hope I have made you proud. I love you with all of my heart.

My mom for always putting the right resources in my hands, and for reading to me since I was a little girl. I will always remember the magic of the library, thank you for imparting your love of books to me.

Bean, for translating beautifully what I saw in my mind onto this cover. Your work never fails to impress and captivate. I have no doubt you will go far. Thank you for helping me understand the struggles I was experiencing when it came to my writing, you helped me appreciate what it means to be a creative. I love you, kiddo.

Chris, for being my sounding board whenever I needed to work through an idea. Every time I doubted myself, you reminded me I could do this and reassured me what an amazing writer I am. You never once faltered in your belief in me. Thank you for supporting my dream, I love you honey bear.

Last, I tried to include this late in my second draft and could not find the right spot, so a little inside joke that I envisioned Ford saying to Peri: What is the Devil's Dream? Mosquitos. Hikers who know, know.

—Kimberly Wheelock, 5/2/23

ABOUT THE AUTHOR

Kimberly Wheelock lives in the Pacific Northwest with Mount Rainier in her backyard. She prefers to experience the outdoors whenever possible and will tell you her best ideas come when she is hiking in the middle of the forest. She is both a writer and reader of genre fiction, can't pass up a potato if it's on the menu, and wants to be a detective when she grows up. Her short story "The Impression of Leaves" won the Elizabeth Breen Prose Award in 2009. WONDERLAND is her first full length novel.

Contact at kimberlywheelockwrites@gmail.com

www.kimberlywheelockwrites.com

@kimberlywheelock_writes

@kimberlywheelock_writes

www.ingramcontent.com/pod-product-compliance
Lightning Source LLC
Chambersburg PA
CBHW020039310726
48970CB00007B/2325